*Time passes
and the world changes.
The remains of the past
are shrouded
in uncertainty.*

—MATSUO BASHO

RINGS OF GRASS

NANCY HEDBERG

LIVING BOOKS
Tyndale House Publishers, Inc.
Wheaton, Illinois

First printing, Living Books edition, July 1985

Library of Congress Catalog Card Number 85-50299
ISBN 0-8423-5605-3
Copyright © 1985 by Nancy Hedberg
Printed in the United States of America

CONTENTS

1 TWO WOMEN

The door handle squeaked and then the church door itself ground open.

Maggie moved away from the coffin and hurriedly pulled her gloves from her handbag, her eyelids flickering in irritation at the sight of her bandaged hand. So stupid. Her mother had always told her to be cautious with broken glass.

A woman's high heels clicked in the entryway. When Maggie turned and saw the startled look on the woman's face as she entered the sanctuary, she was grateful she had heard her coming and had taken a moment to compose herself. She had to admit it probably seemed peculiar for her to be there.

But Lars would have understood why she had to come today. Lars would have understood a lot of things.

Maybe.

Maybe not.

Maybe that was just part of the myth—like so many other things.

There was a large bouquet of yellow chrysanthemums at the front of the sanctuary and the plaque next to the coffin had his name in cold black letters: Lars Graham Engles.

She should have forgotten about him long ago. By now he should have become a vague memory, his words and face blending together in a carefree collage of youth. Instead his words were branded upon her brain, like a message etched again and again.

"I love you more than anything. . . ."

She had mentally traced his words, seeking to understand their meaning, trying to fit them in with all the other words, trying to hear them all again and believe them. She wanted it to be the way it was—the way she had thought it was.

". . . except my God."

The woman was walking to the front of the sanctuary, the old wooden floor creaking beneath her shoes. As she approached she glanced from Maggie's face to the coffin and then back to her face again. When Maggie looked into the woman's eyes she expected to see confusion, even anger. Instead her eyes were softened in sympathy.

"You must be Maggie," the woman said.

"Y . . . yes," Maggie replied. "And you . . . you're Samantha?"

The woman nodded. "And really," Samantha said, "I think I'd have recognized you anywhere. Lars told me so much about you."

"Really? Oh, well, Lars mentioned you too . . . I

mean, I guess it was you." Maggie stopped, embarrassed, then blundered on. "He didn't mention your name—just that he was thinking of getting married."

Samantha laughed lightly. "Yes, it must have been me. Lars really hasn't had that many women in his life, you know."

Maggie lifted her chin slightly. "Well, no, I didn't know," she said quickly.

Samantha touched her on the sleeve. "I'm sorry, Maggie, that was a silly thing to say."

Maggie blinked her eyes rapidly. It was all wrong. Everything was wrong. Even the coffin. Tan. It should have been gray. She wondered for a moment who had picked it out. Mr. Engles? Or was it Samantha? Surely they knew Lars better than that.

She wasn't being fair. Not fair expecting others to think about things like color as she and Lars had done—thought they'd done. But they had both known—had been so sure.

He had turned to her as they lay in the sun on the beach and asked, "What color am I?"

"Gray," she'd said. "What color am I?"

"Yellow."

And they had looked into each other's eyes and laughed and hugged each other because it was so true. He was gray—gentle, serious gray—and she was yellow. Without him she was too bright. Without her he was funereal.

They had been so sure.

She closed her eyes and reached for the casket to steady herself. She felt the cold enamel of Lars's coffin beneath her fingers and she wanted to lock into forever all the fleeting moments that had slipped away from her over the years. She stood there, blind, beside his coffin, her hand roving back and forth across the shiny surface . . . until the presence of the other woman pressed into her reverie and she was forced to open her eyes and return to the present. She moved a few inches away from the casket.

"Well, I suppose . . . I suppose I should be going," Maggie said. She was putting on her gloves as she spoke—anxious to cover up the bandage on her hand, watching her hands carefully to make sure she got the right fingers in the right holes. She performed the rite slowly, as he had done so long ago—only in reverse.

They had sat in this very church, their hands hidden beneath the hymnbook—and he had taken off her white glove, making tiny tugs on the end of each finger until her hand was free and they could feel the skin of each other's hands and entwine their fingers. They had stared at the words in the hymnal and moved their lips as though singing. All the while they had thought only of their hands and how they felt against each other. She had silently prayed that the minister would lead the congregation through all five stanzas.

Maggie smelled the faint bitter aroma of the chrysanthemums and glanced at Samantha, who was moving toward her as if intending to touch her again. "It was good of you to come, Maggie," Samantha said, extending her hand.

Maggie's cheeks flushed in sudden anger and she backed away involuntarily. Who gave

Samantha the right to decide whether or not it was good of her to come? Maggie took several steps down the aisle, then turned to face the other woman. She let her eyes move from Samantha's face to the still form in the coffin, and then to the bouquet of yellow flowers. "Lars would have loved the flowers," she said, her voice slow and deliberate. "Yellow was his favorite color."

"It was?" Samantha said. "I didn't know that."

Maggie nodded her head and stared into Samantha's eyes. "He always loved yellow," she said. "It reminded him of sunshine." They stared at each other in silence.

Still warm with anger, but wanting to black out the other woman's presence, Maggie stepped back to the coffin and permitted Lars's words to form inside her mind another time—clear words, the handwriting squarish, half print, half script.

"I cannot see you anymore. . . ."

And something about his God. She had thought she understood them both—Lars and his God. She had even believed that his God was her God. How could she have thought that? How could she have believed that the God of Abraham, Isaac, Jacob—and Lars—could also be the God of Margaret—Maggie?

She reached her hand toward Lars's crinkled face; then, remembering Samantha was watching her every move, she drew it back. She caressed the lined face with her eyes. *"I'm committed to you, Maggie. I am. Forever."*

It still didn't make sense. Perhaps it never would. By now Lars was cavorting around heaven with his beloved God. She was left behind with a garbled mass of memories that, no matter how many ways she put them together, didn't make sense. Like a myth.

But myths didn't have to make sense.

Where had she heard that? Somewhere.

She turned to the other woman and stared at her in silence. "Good-bye, Samantha," she said at last.

"Good-bye, Maggie."

2 RINGS AND VOWS

✿

Maggie hurried from the church, her footsteps echoing in her ears like reverberations inside a hollow cave—a tomb.

Once outside the door she squinted her eyes against the fading afternoon sunlight and paused to catch her breath. She couldn't see the bay from there, even on her tiptoes. But above the misty treetops along the shore she could see the trees on the neighboring island. Shaw Island, she supposed. Or was it Lopez? She took the surrounding islands for granted and was never sure where one island ended and another began—so many bays, peninsulas, and channels.

Before starting down the steps, Maggie looked across the valley in the opposite direction. Out there, somewhere, was Haro Strait, and beyond that the icy waters of the Pacific. Cattle Point, the southernmost part of San Juan, was about ten miles away, although it seemed much farther because of the narrow, twisting roads. Roche Harbor, at the other end of the island, was about the same distance to the north. Maggie had lived on San Juan all her life. She was used to a life bordered on every side by the rhythm of the cold, restless waters.

She let her eyes fall on the headstones in the cemetery that sloped down the hill behind the church. Lars would be put there soon—buried beside his mother in the cold, soggy earth.

When Maggie arrived home she fixed herself a cup of hot tea and carried it into the living room. The house was quiet. Her husband, Andrew, was still at work, and his sister, Rachel, and her children were out at her in-laws' house for dinner.

The children's sleeping bags were rolled up in the corner. Would Annie and Peter attend the funeral? They were awfully young—about the age she'd been when her father had died. She hadn't gone.

But that was different. Lars wasn't their father. He wasn't anyone's father.

She sat on the couch sipping her tea while the evening shadows crept into the house. Her tea grew cold.

Something soft brushed her leg and she reached down to scratch her old gray cat. "Are you hungry, girl?" she asked. "Are you hungry?" But still she sat in the gathering darkness. "Come on, Pippin," she said at last. "I'll get you some milk."

She poured the milk into the dish and watched Pippin lap it greedily. "You're getting fat, Pippin. I should put you on a diet." When Pippin had finished her milk, Maggie lifted her into her arms and held the cat close to her neck, running her fingers through the soft gray fur.

Even though Lars was dead, the questions were still there—all the questions she'd tried to smother over the years. Maybe after Lars was buried the questions would cease. Maybe the spirits of the dead really did linger on earth for a few days before going to wherever it is they go.

Pippin squirmed in her arms. Maggie put her down, then opened the door to let her go outside. After shutting the door she stood with her hand on the knob for a moment. Then Maggie went into the pantry and searched for her flashlight. She found it behind a bottle of ammonia.

She made her way through the garage and up into the attic. The circle of light danced over a broken table, some buckets of paint, and a bumper from their '64 Chevrolet.

The box she was looking for was hidden in a dark corner. It was covered with dust and smelled of mildew. She carried the box downstairs and into her bedroom. After blowing the dust off the lid, Maggie opened the box and stared at the remains of Lars G. Engles—the real remains. She lifted the box and turned it upside down, dumping the contents onto the bed. She dropped the box to the floor and sat on the bed beside the pile of souvenirs. Wallowing. She knew she was—but she didn't care.

She ran her fingers through the memorabilia— a token from the penny arcade, snapshots of Lars, and one of her and Lars together, arm in arm. She wasn't sure what she was looking for—until she found it. It was a little ring of dried grass. Maggie carefully lifted it from among the other relics.

She fingered the ring delicately, then slipped it over the tip of her ring finger and slid it back and forth between her knuckle and fingernail. She didn't try to slip it over her joint. Her hand was still swollen from the cuts and the ring was fragile. Even as she touched it, pieces of dry grass broke off. She was amazed that it still existed at all.

Grass, of all things.

Lars had taken that into consideration. He had explained it to her carefully. "This ring is temporal," he had said. "But it's not the ring that's important. It's the words we are saying to each other." He even had a Bible verse. He *always* had a Bible verse. "The grass withereth, the flower fadeth; but the word of our God shall stand forever." Then he had prayed—calling upon God to seal their words with the same permanence with which he had sealed his own Word.

Maggie stared at the ring on her finger and took a deep breath. She let the air back out again. There wasn't enough room in her chest for her heart and her lungs and all that excess air. Her heart was expanding, beating heavily, pressing against her lungs and crowding up into her throat.

If the ring still existed—this fragile, dried, withered ring—then surely the words they had murmured into the wind high above the rolling surf also existed.

Somewhere they were etched in stone.

They had spent the day at Cattle Point, on the south end of the island. In the morning they had investigated the landmarks commemorating the infamous Pig War—a thirteen-year war between the United States and England whose only casualty was a British pig. Both the British and American camps had been turned into state parks. The British camp on the north end of the island was lush and serene, nestled into a tiny cove. But the American camp at Cattle Point, on the southern tip of the island, was a barren grassland riddled with rabbit burrows.

But there was a beautiful sandy beach along the eastern shore and Maggie and Lars spent the afternoon there—lying in the sun, kissing and teasing each other, and basking in the pleasure and communion of their young bodies.

By late afternoon they had both felt a little wild—distracted—as if the world they were in was not quite real. Maggie's face was flushed and her eyes were bright when she pulled away from him. When Lars spoke his voice was husky. His eyes wandered to the cape at the tip of the island.

"How about climbing up to the lighthouse?" he said. "We haven't done that for a long time."

Maggie raised herself to a sitting position and ran her fingers through her hair. She cleared her throat. "Good idea," she said.

They gathered their picnic gear and headed down the beach toward the trail leading to the top of the cape. The climb was awkward and tiring, especially with their picnic basket and blanket; but when they reached the top the view was glorious.

The strait was a deep, sparkling blue. The sky was a lighter blue with thin, layered clouds stretched across the horizon. It was June and the grass in the meadow below the lighthouse was still cool and green.

"Oh, it's beautiful," Maggie whispered. She let the blanket she held in her arms fall to the ground. She stooped over, unstrapping her sandals. Then, glancing back at Lars, she said, "I'll bet you can't catch me." She darted through the grass.

Lars stared at her a moment and then dropped their picnic basket. He charged after her. "You're going to be sorry," he said.

"Why?" she called back.

"Because," he bellowed, "you don't know who I am."

Maggie spun around, teasing him. "Who are you?" she asked.

Lars crouched low, ready to lunge at Maggie. "I'm the Mugger," he said. "And I'm going to get you."

Maggie darted away. "Oh, no, you're not!" She ran through the tall grass, zigzagging widely to stay out of Lars's reach.

As Maggie ran she savored the feel of the grass against her bare legs, and the breeze, with barely a hint of its usual salty bite, against her cheeks. Her foot slipped into a rabbit burrow and she nearly fell. But she regained her balance in time to move once again out of Lars's reach.

"I almost got you that time," Lars shouted into the salty breeze. His voice was ragged and he sounded out of breath. He was gaining on her.

She spun around again, crouching low, her hand warding him off. She backed away from him. He crouched opposite her, his hands on his knees. He was trying to leer, but was gasping for breath instead.

"You're already pooping out," Maggie hollered, her own voice breathless and weak.

"Watch your language!"

"What language?" Maggie asked.

"Pooping," he said. "That's no way for a lady to talk."

Maggie was eyeing him closely, watching for a chance to dart to one side and once again escape his reach. She continued to back away from him. "Well, maybe I'm not a lady."

"Oh, yes, you are," he said. "You're a lady, all right." He moved toward her, his back bent and his arms reaching out toward her. "But I'm going to take care of that!"

Maggie moved slowly from side to side and suddenly dashed to the right. Lars lunged for her and caught the tail of her shirt. Maggie swung her arm against Lars's hand and the momentum was enough for him to lose his grip on her shirt. She darted away again. But she could hear Lars's footsteps close behind her.

A quiver ran through her abdomen and into her legs.

Soon she heard his panting, and then she felt his breath, warm against her neck. She made a final lunge away from him, but in a moment his arms were around her and he had pulled her to the ground.

She closed her eyes and pounded her fists

against his chest. "Brute, brute," she said. But then she let her head fall back, and she could feel her hair becoming tangled in the sticky grass. She could feel the soft earth beneath her body and the warmth of the sun against her bare legs.

In the distance she could hear the rolling of the waves in the bay. Then for a moment she felt Lars's strong, lean body stretched tight against her own. She opened her eyes and looked into his face. His eyes were serious and gentle. The laughter drained from her own eyes and she lifted her lips to his. Lars pressed his mouth against hers in a kiss as insistent as it was tender.

Lars and Maggie came together without quite realizing it was what they had intended all along. They made love in the sticky, green grass at the top of the cape with the sun caressing their bodies, and with the sound of the bay and the throb of their own passion pounding against their ears. They poured into each other all their love and dreams and sorrow of longings. And afterwards they lay exhausted in the shimmering fragments of their childhood dreams.

Maggie began to weep.

Lars held her face against his neck. "Oh, Maggie," he said, "I'm sorry. I . . . I didn't mean for that to happen, really I didn't." He closed his eyes, and as he spoke his voice was low and intense. The muscles in his face were pulled tightly across his cheeks. "Maggie . . . Maggie, I love you so much." He shook his head from side to side. ". . . Way too much."

Maggie pressed her fingers into his shoulders. She let her head fall back onto the grass. Lars knelt over her and caressed her face with his fingers. "Maggie," he said. "Maggie . . . look at me. Please. Look at me."

Maggie looked into his eyes.

"Maggie, I. . . ." He bit his lip and his eyes became shiny and more startling in their blueness. "I know you gave yourself to me because you love me and . . . and because you trust me," he said. "I'm going to marry you, Maggie."

Maggie closed her eyes and squeezed them together tightly. The remaining tears were forced out the corners of her eyes, and they slid across her temples and disappeared into her tangled mass of hair. "Lars, don't. . . ."

"I mean now, Maggie," Lars said. "Right now." Maggie kept her eyes closed. "Maggie. My God, Maggie, *look* at me. Please at least look at me!"

Maggie opened her eyes, but when she looked into Lars's face her body convulsed in a giant sob.

Lars pulled her to a sitting position and gathered her into his arms. She clung to him, sobbing. Lars pulled away from Maggie and placed his hands on her shoulders, looking into her face. Then he took one of her hands in both of his, caressing it softly as he spoke. "What does it mean to be married?" he asked solemnly.

Maggie wiped her cheeks with the back of her free hand. She shrugged her shoulders. "You know—living together, having babies, in sickness and in health—all of that."

"But what does it mean, really? If we didn't live together and we didn't have babies—for a while at least—what would it mean for us to be married to each other?"

"Well . . . well, I guess it would mean that we were—" She swept her hand back and forth between them. "You know, promised to each other—committed."

Lars leaned forward earnestly. "I am that," he said. His face was solemn and his eyes brimmed with tenderness.

"Well, me too, but. . . ."

"Maggie, there will never be anyone else for me—ever. I want to . . . I want you to know that."

Maggie shook her head. "Lars, I know you wouldn't. . . ."

Lars took both her hands and pressed them to his lips. "Maggie, Maggie, listen to me. I know you. You're going to get frightened. . . . I know you are—so am I." He leaned forward and looked intently into her face. "I need to know that we are committed to each other—before God—forever."

"But we are, Lars, we are. I know that."

"But don't you see? We need a ritual or something."

Maggie smiled. "Well . . . I don't know if this was a ritual exactly, but. . . ."

"Maggie, please—" He lowered his head, shaking it slowly from side to side.

She stared at his sober face. "Lars, I'm sorry. I didn't mean to. . . . You're really serious, aren't you?"

Lars lifted his head and looked into her eyes. "I want . . . I want to have a ceremony right here. Right here in this meadow—you, me, and God. I want to commit myself to you forever . . . and I want God to witness it, and. . . ."

Maggie gazed into his eyes. "You mean, you

want us to be married—before God—to let God marry us? But. . . ."

"Someday we'll be married legally, with the relatives and the cake and all of that . . . but this, this will be our real wedding. Do you understand what I'm saying?"

Maggie nodded her head. "But, Lars, if . . . well, this is serious. What if one of us changes his mind?"

Lars shook his head.

Maggie shook her head also, almost automatically, as if her head was invisibly attached to his. "It's forever?"

"It's forever." He pulled his eyebrows together. "Maggie, it's forever anyway—at least for me it is. I always thought it was for you, too."

She nodded her head.

Lars took her hand in his once again. "Will you marry me?"

"Yes," Maggie whispered.

She was thoughtful for a moment. "I'll need a bouquet," she said, smiling. She stood up and glanced about. Then she ran off to gather a handful of grasses and wild flowers. When she returned, Lars was kneeling on the ground, carefully braiding some grass together into a tiny circle.

"A triple strand, not easily broken," he said. Maggie imagined he was quoting a Bible verse, as usual.

She knelt beside him, and after watching him for a few moments, she pulled some of the nearby grass and began weaving a ring also. When they were finished they laid the rings side by side on a

cloth napkin from their picnic basket. Maggie
tried to fasten some flowers to Lars's T-shirt for a
boutonniere. She finally gave up and stuck a
flower behind one of his ears. He left it there.
Maggie held the remaining grasses and flowers in
her hand as she would have held the finest bridal
bouquet. They looked into each other's eyes and
then knelt before the napkin and their braided
rings. "Let's pray first," Lars said.

Maggie nodded.

"Dear Father," Lars began, "we love each other.
We want to spend the rest of our lives together.
And today we want to promise ourselves to each
other. Please witness our vows—cement them. In
Jesus' name, amen."

Lars turned to her. "Maggie," he said, "I love
you. I promise to be faithful to you forever. There
will never be anyone else but you. I will cherish
you and protect you in sickness and in health, in
richness or poverty, in good times and bad times.
I am committed to you forever. I promise." He
slipped the tiny braided ring on her finger.

There was a slight pause and then Maggie's
voice broke into the silence against the quiet
thunder of the distant waves. "Lars, I love you
with all my heart. I will be faithful to you and will
love and respect you all the days of my life. I will
remain by your side in good times and bad
times." Her voice increased in its fervency. "I will
mother your children and will stay with you
always, a faithful helpmeet, friend, and lover. I
promise." As she slid the grass ring onto his
finger, a strand of grass loosed itself and she
paused to tuck it neatly back into the braid.

They stared at each other in silence for a moment before Lars tilted her chin upward and they kissed a solemn kiss of love and devotion. Then they lay down together in the grass and held each other close. Maggie shivered and Lars pulled her closer to himself, pressing her face against his cheek.

3 COLLEGE

Maggie stared at the tiny grass ring she held in her fingers. It was dry and brittle. She imagined the rings as they had been long ago—side by side on the cloth napkin. Lars had braided his tightly and evenly. She had braided hers awkwardly, pieces of grass sticking out in the wrong places. She could remember how the ring had felt—cool and flexible—as Lars had slipped it onto her finger.

Strange. As vivid as the ceremony atop the cape remained in Maggie's mind, she and Lars had never discussed it afterward. Not once. It was not clear to Maggie whether the ceremony had been too silly to talk about—or too holy—but it had remained a mysteriously taboo subject.

The September following their pseudomarriage, Maggie and Lars had left for college in Seattle. Except for occasional short trips to the mainland, they had spent their entire lives on the tiny island of San Juan.

Travel to and from the island was done by water or air. The islanders were used to having their travel schedules regulated by the coming and going of the ferries.

Lars's father took Maggie and Lars on the ferry from San Juan to Vancouver Island. Then he drove them from Sydney to Victoria where Lars and Maggie boarded the ferry for Seattle. Mr. Engles shook Lars's hand and gave Maggie a big hug. They waved to him as the ferry moved away from the dock.

When Maggie and Lars stepped from the ferry onto the Seattle wharf, the stench of the harbor and the vastness of the city intoxicated them. They sucked the putrid air into their lungs and looked into each other's eyes with longing and a certain wildness—they felt loosed and un-shackled.

They took a bus from the wharf to the small Bible college. When they reached the tree-shaded campus, it was like another little island—a center of purity and truth within a larger world of freedom and squalor.

The first week was chaotic. They went through orientation, registered for classes, and passed judgment on new roommates. But by the second week things were beginning to make sense. Maggie and Lars were settling into the order of things and familiarizing themselves with various college codes—written and unwritten.

The moral code at the college was unwritten—but simple and clear. There were not ten commandments—only one: "Thou shalt not have sex outside of marriage." Even their intimate ceremony atop the cape could not relieve the guilt Lars and Maggie felt at having transgressed the moral code.

They tried to align themselves with the ideals of their youth and with the moral stance of the Bible-dominated campus. But they were as two people possessed—as if, having drunk the love potion, they were helpless to resist.

Still, they tried.

Whenever they had sex they were careful to remind each other that it must not happen again. They regularly made love in the supply room of the music building where Lars was a part-time janitor, and sometimes they made love in the backseats of borrowed cars. But it was not something they planned.

It just happened.

"Where'd you get it?" Maggie asked, walking around the car, trying to inspect it like an expert.

"I borrowed it from Fred," Lars said. "It's nothing fancy, but it sure beats walking."

"Sure does." Maggie poked her head through the open window and scrutinized the interior. Her eyes traveled slowly over the backseat.

"Well, where shall we go tonight?" Lars asked.

"Tonight? He's going to let you use it on a Friday night?"

Lars tipped forward and back, from his heels to his toes to his heels. "Yep. What do you want to do?"

"Um . . . I don't know. What do you want to do?"

Lars pulled her toward him. He thought a moment. "How about going to the Chinese Terrace for dinner?"

Maggie and Lars didn't dine out often—Lars couldn't afford it—but when they did, they usually went to the Chinese Terrace. It was less expensive than most of the American restaurants, and it seemed exotic sipping Chinese tea and practicing with chopsticks. But it was the fortune cookies they liked best. They didn't believe in the fortunes, of course, but Maggie had one on her bulletin board that promised a lasting love and many children.

"What does it say?" Maggie asked, trying to peek over Lars's shoulder.

"Just a minute. I haven't had a chance to read it yet." He held the fortune away from her so she couldn't see it. "It might be private."

"If it's genuine, it won't be private. Any real fortune cookie would know we are destined for each other and that we don't have any 'privates' from each other."

Lars furrowed his brow. "You talk funny." He held the tiny paper at arm's length and squinted at it. "It says, my dear," he said dramatically, "that I should beware of sexy women wearing," he pulled up the tablecloth and peered under the table, "black leather pumps."

"Let me see that!" she said, trying to grab it from him.

"No, no, no," he said, holding it away from her.

She put her elbows on the table and rested her chin in her hands. Then she tilted her head and smiled at him. "Did you say sexy?" She fluffed her hair with her hand.

Lars glanced at her quickly. "Oh, no. No, I'm sorry," he said, holding up his hand. "That's not right. I read that wrong." He held out the tiny slip of paper and once again peered at it soberly. "*Sixty* women," he said. "Beware of *sixty* women wearing black leather pumps."

Maggie laughed. "What does it really say?"

"Well," Lars said, repeating his dramatic performance, "It says, 'The remains of the past are shrouded in uncertainty.' "

Maggie lowered her eyelids and murmured, "Obscure, very obscure."

"What does yours say?" Lars asked.

Maggie cracked open the crusty cookie and pulled out the thin yellow paper. "It says," she read, " 'Come to a quick decision regarding a puzzling situation.' "

"Aha," Lars said, pounding the table. "We don't have much time."

"To what?"

"To decide what we're going to do next."

As he spoke he pressed her fingers against his lips. She allowed him to kiss her fingertips absently. "What are our options?" she inquired.

"Well, we can either observe the rich or we can observe the poor. Which shall we do first?"

"Who are the rich?"

"The people in the lobby of the Olympic Hotel."

"And the poor?"

"The winos on First Avenue."

Maggie paused briefly. "The poor," she said. "The poor it is."

"I hope I can remember how to get there," Lars said as he stopped at a light.

Maggie glanced at the map in her hand and then the signpost. "Well, this is Sixth and Pike," she said. "If you keep going you should come right to it."

"Something doesn't seem right," Lars said as he pulled away from the light.

At the next corner Maggie said, "Lars, this is Seventh. You're going the wrong way."

"But it's a one-way street. I can only go one way."

"Then you're on the wrong street."

Lars looked around in confusion and then pulled over to the curb. He turned to Maggie, putting his arm around her shoulder. He nuzzled his nose into her hair. "I can't concentrate," he said. He lifted her chin with his hand and looked into her eyes. Then he kissed her long and passionately.

Maggie wiggled and pulled herself free. "Pine!" she said.

"Peppermint."

"What?"

"My toothpaste. It's peppermint, not pine."

Maggie threw back her head and laughed. "No, no, no. The street. We're supposed to be on Pine, not Pike. Pine goes the other way."

"Oh, well, pardon me," he said, glancing over his shoulder. He reached around Maggie to put the car in gear. "I didn't mean to interrupt your little tour here. Sheesh. Two hundred and seventy-eight girls on campus and I end up with a travel guide!"

"It was your idea to go see the bums," Maggie reminded him, unperturbed.

"Bums, smums."

"Here, Lars, turn here," Maggie shouted as he drove through the intersection. She turned around and looked out the back window. "You missed it," she said.

"She's a prophet, too," he muttered.

"Lars. . . ."

"I'm just kidding."

"You are not."

"I am too."

"You are not. You're pouting."

"I am not pouting."

"Then why is your lower lip so big?"

"Passion. Passion makes my lower lip get big."

Maggie peered at him. "That's not passion," she said. "I know passion when I see it."

Lars stopped at the next intersection and glanced around in confusion. Then he turned to Maggie and looked her full in the face. She looked up at him, laughing, but then her face grew sober, her eyes shiny. "Oh, Lars. . . ."

A car honked behind them.

"Drat! Where in the world are we?"

Maggie glanced at the street signs. "This is Tenth. Turn to the left at the next corner. The next street should be Pine. Then go back the way we came."

Lars turned left, and then to the left again. The streets grew darker and the neighborhoods seedier. When Lars finally turned onto First Avenue, Maggie stared in amazement. The streets were littered with bottles and brown paper bags,

and winos hung out in doorways. Maggie and
Lars drove past the bars and dance halls, trying to
catch an occasional glimpse inside as the doors
opened and people staggered out. Signs in the
windows were glaring and crude. TOPLESS
GO-GO GIRLS. NUDE ON STAGE. NOW APPEAR-
ING: FANNY LAMOUR.

"Oh, look at that poor man," Maggie said,
pointing to a wino slouched on the sidewalk
against a grimy brick building. He was wearing a
black suit jacket, brown slacks, and hiking boots.
His shirt was a green-gray color. Something about
the color of his shirt unnerved Maggie. It
suggested the vulgar details of the man's story—
all the forgotten times and places of a soiled life.

"Doesn't he have any place else to sleep?"

"Probably not."

As Lars drove down the street, Maggie took in
the old stone buildings with their grimy windows.
There were men lingering in dark doorways and
loitering on the street corners. Occasionally she
would catch sight of someone staring blankly out
of a second story window—a dim yellow light
bulb burning in the background, dank curtains
hanging against the windowpane.

"How come there aren't any women bums?"

"Huh?"

"They're all men. Aren't there any lady bums?"

"Lady bums, my dear, are called prostitutes."

"All of them?"

Lars shrugged his shoulders. "I guess so."

"That seems funny."

"They have something they can sell," Lars said,
shrugging his shoulders again, "so they sell it."

"It still seems funny."

They drove down First Avenue several times.

"Want to go in there, Maggie?" Lars asked, pointing to one of the topless bars.

"Sure."

"They wouldn't let you in."

"Why?"

"You're too nice," he said, putting his arm around her. "You would blind them with your purity and virtue."

"Right."

They cruised down First Avenue one more time, then Lars asked, "Have you seen enough?"

Maggie nodded her head.

"Well, are you ready to observe the rich?"

Maggie leaned her head against his shoulder. "I guess so," she said.

When they walked into the lobby of the Olympic Hotel, the quiet dignity of the old building with its burnished gold carpet, soft leather chairs, and ornate chandeliers contrasted startlingly with the squalor of First Avenue. They stood still for a few moments, taking in the graceful stairway and the ornate balustrades of the balcony overlooking the lobby. It was nearly deserted.

"I don't see any rich people," Maggie said.

"I know," Lars said, glancing about. "I guess we'll have to resort to plan B."

"Plan B?"

"Just go along with everything I do," Lars said. "When you figure out what we're doing, we'll leave. OK?"

Maggie looked at him skeptically, but agreed.

Lars put his arm around her, pulled her close, and led her across the lobby. When he passed the main entrance he waved grandly at the surprised bellhop. The bellhop waved feebly back.

"Grand chap," Lars confided to Maggie.

As they passed the main desk, Lars nodded at the clerk. "Fine evening, sir," he said in a deep voice.

"Yes, sir," the clerk responded, not sure whether or not to take him seriously.

Maggie started to giggle.

"Ah, your laughter, my love, is like music to my soul," Lars said, "and your lips are like a scarlet thread. Come with me." He led her to the broad staircase that curved its way to the mezzanine. As they walked slowly up the stairs, Lars pressed his lips against Maggie's ear and said, "Your eyes are like doves."

Maggie laughed. "That's my ear."

Lars continued. "Your neck is like a tower of ivory, the fragrance of your breath like. . . ."

"Stop," Maggie said, pulling away from him. "I've got it." They were at the top of the stairs and they paused, facing each other. "Easy," she said. "We're acting out the Song of Solomon."

Lars laughed. "Nope. That's not it." He stroked his chin. "But that's good. That's very good. I'll have to remember that."

"I'm sure you will." Maggie laughed.

Lars glanced around. The mezzanine was deserted. "Just a minute," he said. He led her to a couch tucked away in a corner beneath a dark painting in a huge gilt frame. "OK, here we go again," he said. "Keep guessing."

He glanced around and then pulled Maggie into a tight embrace, kissing her long and hard. Maggie resisted at first, and then gave in to him. When he let her go she gasped, "You're a mad rapist and I'm . . . I'm the helpless victim."

Lars laughed. "I may be a mad rapist," he said, "but you are hardly a helpless victim." He shook his head. "Nope. That's not it." He glanced around again. "Well, we'll just have to keep trying, I guess." He pulled her toward himself and kissed her once again. Then he snuggled his lips against her ear and whispered, "Well, how does it feel to be Mrs. Engles, Mrs. Engles?"

Maggie pulled away. "Aha! We're on our honeymoon."

Lars planted tiny kisses all around her mouth. "That's right," he whispered. He held her tightly and kissed her on the neck.

"Lars . . . we're in public . . . this is no way. . . . Lars!"

"They understand," he murmured. "Didn't you see the bellhop and the desk clerk? They know we're on our honeymoon. Everyone understands."

"But, Lars," she said, moving her face from side to side to avoid his kisses, "we can stop pretending now. I guessed it. Lars. . . ." He kept kissing her. "If we're on our honeymoon," Maggie said, finally managing to release herself from his arms, "what are we doing here? Why aren't we in our room?" She patted her hair and tried to smooth her skirt.

"Because," Lars said, leaning over her, trying to find her lips once again, "the maid is cleaning it."

"Um . . . I see." He pressed his lips against hers

and, after hesitating briefly, she returned his kiss, submitting herself to his arms, allowing her body to melt against his.

Lars pulled away from her. "Come with me," he said. He took her by the hand and led her to the stairwell and up one flight of stairs. The second story hallway was deserted and dimly lit. Lars led her by the hand down the hall and around the nearest corner. Then once again he pulled her into his arms and kissed her.

Maggie was lost in the warmth of his embrace. Her face was flushed and her eyes were bright. "I think," she murmured, "I think the maid had better hurry up with that room."

Lars groaned and pressed his lips against her ear. "Let's go to the car," he said.

Their lovemaking was no longer that of awkward beginners. Now the only awkwardness was that of cramped quarters. Afterward they sat huddled together in the backseat, their coats thrown over them, basking in their closeness.

But it was a nippy evening and the outside chill began to creep into the car. Lars started the engine. They sat in silence waiting for the car to warm up.

Then they began talking, quietly and soberly. They reminded each other that they must never let it happen again.

Maggie cried.

Lars apologized.

4 UPHEAVAL

ᘒᘒᘒᘒ

It was October and the leaves had turned from green to gold. Already they were littering the campus beneath the big old trees. Suddenly posters appeared around campus.

SPIRITUAL EMPHASIS WEEK
Speaker: Dr. Ralph Trimble
Special Music
November 2-6
Prepare for a Blessing!

Maggie pondered how to prepare for a blessing. Blessings didn't have to be prepared for. Only disasters. "Who's this Dr. Trimble?" she asked Lars one day on their way to the lunchroom.

"I don't know. Never heard of him."

"I hope he's not boring."

"I wouldn't count on it."

Dr. Ralph Trimble was a lot of things, but boring wasn't one of them. He hit the campus like a storm. Students, parents, faculty, and staff were agog. Nobody knew who or what he was going to attack next.

He was against television and for Bible reading. He thought family devotions were usually a joke, but was highly in favor of fasting. He spoke lightly of doorbell-ringing, button-wearing, sloganeering evangelists, but understood those who ministered in bars. He turned the campus upside down.

Students who had long planned to become missionaries decided to stay home and befriend their neighbors instead. Boys who had dreamed of becoming professional football players suddenly felt called to shed God's light in deep, dark Africa. Girls previously desiring to be Christian wives and mothers now spurned the very idea of marriage in favor of becoming full-time brides of Christ. Others, previously reconciled to lonely lives of service for Christ, found themselves with a new assurance that "it was not good for man to be alone."

Assumptions were shattered across the board.

It was as if Dr. Trimble had loosed the campus from its moorings and had cast it into the sea, shouting, "Swim for your lives." He was unmoved by the students' frantic thrashings. "God alone can save you," seemed to be his final message.

Tuesday morning when Maggie returned to the dorm after chapel, she found her roommate, Linda, kneeling beside her bed, sobbing.

"Linda, what's wrong?" Maggie asked, crouching beside her. "What happened?"

Linda shook her head from side to side and continued to sob quietly.

"Linda, tell me what's wrong," Maggie said, pulling the girl to her feet. "What's the matter?"

Linda wiped her nose with the back of her hand. "I have to break up with Mike," she said.

"What? Break up with Mike? But, Linda . . . I thought you and Mike were going to get married!"

"We were."

"Well, what . . . ?"

"God's calling me to be a missionary," she said. "I know he is. And Mike . . . Mike wants to be a schoolteacher."

"Can't he be a missionary schoolteacher?"

Linda shook her head violently and started crying again. "He doesn't want to be a missionary schoolteacher. He wants to stay here, in the United States. He keeps saying, 'First in Jerusalem, then in Judea. . . .' "

"What?"

"You know—start where you are." Linda pulled a tissue from the box on her desk and turned to face the window, her back to Maggie.

"Well . . . maybe he's r. . . ."

Linda shook her head again. "It's not right for me," she said. "I can't explain it. But I know it's not right for me." She rolled her head from side to side and lifted her tragic eyes to Maggie. "But I love him so much," she said. "So much."

Maggie lifted her arms helplessly. "But I don't understand," she said. "If you and Mike love each other, why would God . . . well, why would God call one of you to be a schoolteacher in the U.S. and the other to be a foreign missionary? That doesn't make sense."

Linda blew her nose and shook her head, but

didn't reply. Maggie plopped onto her bed, her chin in her hands. "I don't understand," she said, more to herself than to Linda. She lifted her chin and stared at the ceiling. Her jaw shifted slightly to one side. "It doesn't make sense," she whispered.

Wednesday morning chapel time spilled over into class time as Dr. Trimble declared his truth and as students testified to the changes that were being wrought in their lives.

Linda stood up and told how she felt God calling her to the mission field. Maggie was sitting behind her, and when Linda sat down, Maggie studied her. Linda was composed, but when she turned her head, Maggie could see that her eyes were unusually bright. Her body wasn't rigid, but she sat erect, eagerly watching another student testifying that God was helping him overcome an unnamed bad habit—something to do with the flesh. When he finished, another student arose, and then another. There was a shining intimacy in the Spirit-filled atmosphere of the chapel.

After chapel Maggie rushed to the student union building. She was flushed and out of breath as she glanced around for Lars. When she didn't see him she hurried to claim an empty table. When Lars appeared in the doorway, Maggie's entire body moved involuntarily toward him. As he sat down next to her, her eyes searched his face. She wanted to pull him to herself, back into the intimacy that was theirs alone. She was afraid he might be sucked into that other intimacy—the madness sweeping the campus.

"Hi," she said.

"Hi."

Lars's voice was even and his eyes were distant. But when his gaze met Maggie's he softened. He shifted his eyes back and forth across her face and over her body, warming her like a blanket. And a tiny smile, a smile that was always close by when Maggie was with Lars, began playing around the corners of her mouth. Even Dr. Trimble had not been able to brush it away. Maggie did not laugh out loud, but the laughter was in her—behind her eyes and at the corners of her lips.

Lars cleared his throat. "How did your psych test go this morning?" he asked.

"We didn't have it. Chapel—remember?"

He lowered his eyes. "Oh, that's right."

"What's this about chapel tomorrow?"

"I'm not sure. But they're splitting it—one for the boys, one for the girls."

"That's going too far," Maggie said. "Who does he think he is, anyway?"

Lars didn't reply.

"Why do you think they're doing that?" Maggie asked.

"Fred said Dr. Trimble wants to talk to us separately about . . . well, about sex."

Maggie giggled at his timidity and leaned forward. Her eyes were sparkling with mischief. "For someone who's afraid to talk about it," she said, "you sure can do it!"

"Maggie!" Lars glanced about anxiously.

Maggie's eyes danced at his embarrassment. Her lips were parted slightly and her smiling eyes dared him to resist her. Lars cleared his throat. "Do you want something to eat?"

"Just a cola. Well . . . maybe a side of fries."

He nodded and headed for the counter. When he returned with their order, both their faces were sober.

"What do you think he'll say?" Maggie said.

"You know what he'll say." Lars took a sip of his cola and then put the cup down, his eyes meeting hers.

"But, Lars," she said, "it's different. It's different with us." Her eyes searched his. "I love you so much, it's just . . . it's just . . . what we do is what we are. We're just doing what we are."

Lars shook his head. " 'We're just doing what we are,' " he repeated. "Who would understand talk like that? Nobody talks like that."

"But, Lars," she said, her voice a little higher than usual. "You understand, don't you? I know you understand. It couldn't be if you didn't understand it too."

"I guess so."

"Lars!" Her eyes carried a shadow of fear.

"I understand it," he said. "I'm just not sure Dr. Trimble understands it."

Maggie leaned forward and looked earnestly into Lars's face. "It doesn't matter what Dr. Trimble understands," she said, new resolve filling her words with substance. "Dr. Trimble isn't God. And I know God understands. He does, Lars. I know he does."

Lars met her eyes, but he didn't smile. He nodded his head slightly. "I know God understands," he said. "I'm just not so sure he approves."

Five minutes before the bell for girls' chapel, Lars and Maggie were lingering outside the door, draining the last drop of pleasure from being together. They were leaning against the old brick building, their bodies close together, but not touching. Only their hands were joined.

"I probably won't see you till after our chapel," Lars said.

"I'll wait for you in the lunchroom," Maggie replied.

"OK."

Their fingers were laced together loosely and Maggie moved her fingers lightly against Lars's, working them in and out and back and forth with excruciating pleasure.

Just before the final bell rang, Maggie ducked inside and took her seat in the hushed quiet of the chapel. She crossed her legs and slouched in the seat until her knee touched the back of the row in front of her. Then she turned her attention to the platform.

The student activities coordinator led the girls in two songs and then introduced Dr. Trimble. Dr. Trimble stood silently behind the pulpit a few moments before he began to speak. His huge hands gripped either side of the podium and his eyes traveled solemnly across the faces of the girls before him. He had X-ray vision. He could see through them—exposing their hearts.

As his eyes traveled down Maggie's row, Maggie thought she needed a tissue. She began digging through her purse. What was she looking for? A fingernail file? Couldn't find it. She closed her purse and put it on the floor beneath her seat. By that time Dr. Trimble's eyes had traveled to the back of the auditorium.

"What do you think God thinks of sex?" Dr. Trimble boomed without warning.

The girls sat up in their chairs and stared at him. His eyes traveled slowly over the audience again, examining them silently. Did he expect them to answer? Just as the girls were beginning to shift uneasily, Dr. Trimble leaned forward and shouted, "He loves it!" Then his booming laughter filled the auditorium and the girls stared at each other in amazement. They were afraid to join in his laughter for fear his next statement would once again catch them off guard.

"He loves it," Dr. Trimble repeated quietly. "But because he created it," he continued, wagging his finger at them for emphasis, "he knows all about it. He knows its joys and pleasures; he knows the sorrow and heartbreak that it can cause when it is misused." Dr. Trimble paused and cleared his throat. He took a sip of water from the glass he always kept behind the pulpit. "And that's what I want to talk to you about today—," he said, "the dangers of misused sex."

Maggie pressed one of her thumbs against her right front tooth. She slid her thumb back and forth along the edge of her tooth, which was perfectly smooth. Then she scooted her body back and folded her arms in front of her.

Dr. Trimble explained, quietly and reassuringly,

that the only God-ordained context for sexual intercourse was within the confines of a marriage relationship. "Sexual intercourse outside of marriage is an invitation to disaster," he said loudly, once again examining the faces of the girls with his penetrating blue eyes. This time Maggie didn't lower her eyes. Instead she lifted her chin slightly and stared coldly into the face of Dr. Trimble.

Dr. Trimble leaned forward confidentially. "Unfair as it is," he said, "girls still have more to lose from sex outside of marriage than boys do. Even with modern methods of birth control, the risk of pregnancy exists. And," he said, his voice dark and gravelly, "like it or not, when you girls enter into a sexual relationship with those boys out there, you are exposing yourself to a double standard that the boys themselves deny exists. They won't even admit its reality," he said, waving his arms through the air.

"Never mind all this talk about equality. What boys will excuse in themselves, even Christian boys—perhaps especially Christian boys—they will often not accept in girls. Not the girls they choose to marry." He paused dramatically and took another sip of water.

When he spoke again his voice was nearly shrill. "How can you fight something like that?" he asked. "How can you deal with something every boy you go out with will deny exists?" He leaned forward and shook his head slowly from side to side. "You can't," he said quietly. "You can't. Your only protection is marriage. That's why God ordained marriage. We need marriage to protect us—to protect us from ourselves and from each other."

Protection—from Lars? Maggie sat up straighter in her chair and rested her chin on a closed fist as she stared thoughtfully at Dr. Trimble. She didn't need protection. Lars loved her. That's all that mattered. Lars would never do anything to hurt her. Ever.

"But there's something even more important than that," Dr. Trimble continued. "It has to do with our relationship with God. Do we love God enough to obey him—even when what God wants for us is directly opposed to what we want?"

Maggie frowned and leaned forward. She had noticed that she had a loose thread on the hem of her skirt. She reached down and wound the stray fiber around her index finger. "Because," Dr. Trimble said, wagging his finger at the girls once again, "whatever has become more important to us than obeying God has become our idol." He nodded his head solemnly. "It is all too easy for sex to become an idol. All too easy."

With a quick jerk, Maggie snapped the thread in two. She examined her skirt for any more loose ends, and then, satisfied that everything was in order, she leaned back once more in her chair and folded her arms. She didn't hear another word Dr. Trimble said.

After the lengthy service, Maggie stepped into the chilly November air outside the chapel door and pulled her coat more closely around herself. She stuffed her hands into her coat pockets and walked swiftly toward the dorm. When she was just outside the door of her room she paused. She thought she heard someone weeping. She pushed the door open far enough to peek inside. It was Linda again. She was hunched over her desk, her head on her open Bible, sobbing quietly. Maggie backed away from the door and headed down the hall. She would walk around campus until it was time to meet Lars for lunch.

As she strolled by the old brick buildings and wistfully kicked at the leaves littering the ground, she remembered the grasses and flowers growing in the meadow on the windswept cape high above the strait. She heard Lars's whispered words. *"I'm sorry, Maggie. I . . . I didn't mean for that to happen. I really didn't. I . . . I love you. . . . I want to have a ceremony right here. Right here in this meadow—you, me, and God."*

Maggie tilted her head back and looked into the tree branches overhead. The branches were nearly bare. Here and there leaves still clung to the limbs. Soon they too would give up and the tree branches would stand stark against the winter sky. Naked.

Maggie shivered and walked over to a gnarly oak tree. She leaned against the trunk, shifting her head back until she could feel her hair catch in the scratchy bark. She moved her head back and forth slowly, enjoying the pull of the bark against her thick hair.

"I love you more than anything," he had said. *"Maggie, sometimes . . . sometimes I'm afraid I love you more than I love God."*

She relaxed against the tree and closed her

eyes. It would be OK. Someday they would really get married—with bridesmaids and a minister. Not right away, but soon. Within a year or two. They needed to get their schooling out of the way. Needed their parents' help.

Maggie opened her eyes. She tried to imagine what the bare branches would look like in the spring when tiny little buds appeared to announce the coming of splendid new leaves. She envisioned the branches covered with bright green leaves like those that covered the trees at the edge of the meadow last summer. The leaves would dance and frolic in the breeze. Maggie smiled to herself and glanced at her watch. She shoved herself away from the trunk of the old tree and headed for the lunchroom to wait for Lars.

5 SILENCE

Every time the cafeteria door opened, Maggie looked up expectantly. At first only girls appeared—the boys' chapel was predictably running overtime. But before long a few boys began straggling in. They were more subdued than usual. Some visited quietly with one another, but most of the boys waited silently in line, their faces sober and their bodies still.

As had been true all week, the cafeteria was not crowded. Unannounced prayer meetings had been springing up around campus and it was not unusual for students to spend their lunch hours praying instead of eating. Maggie glanced at her watch. Surely Lars would have let her know if he had decided to go to one of the prayer meetings.

"Hi, Maggie."

Maggie swirled around in her chair, then slouched back in disappointment. It was Lars's roommate, Fred. "Waiting for Lars?"

Maggie nodded her head.

"You might as well go ahead and eat."

"Why do you say that?"

"I saw him talking to Dr. Trimble." Fred shifted his lunch tray to his other hip. "They looked like they were going to be awhile."

Maggie frowned. "What do you mean? What does that look like?"

Fred wrinkled his forehead. "I don't know," he said, shrugging his shoulders. "It just looked that way. Forget it." He shifted his lunch tray again. "Mind if I sit down?"

"Huh? No, go ahead." Maggie shoved a chair away from the table with her foot. Fred set his tray on the table and methodically unloaded its contents onto the tabletop.

Maggie watched in silence while Fred sat down and carefully spread his napkin on his lap, then bowed his head for a silent prayer. As soon as he lifted his head, Maggie said, "You're supposed to pray first."

"I did."

"I mean, you're supposed to pray before you put your napkin on your lap."

"Who says?"

"It's in the Bible."

Fred gave her a crooked look.

Maggie shrugged her shoulders and laughed. "I don't know. I heard it somewhere—some etiquette course I took." She rested her chin on her hand thoughtfully. "It's pretty important, don't you think?"

"Yes," Fred said, waving his roll through the air to emphasize his words. "That is definitely one thing I would not want to go through life not practicing—prayer before napkins. I'll remember that."

The cafeteria door opened and Maggie glanced up quickly, then turned her attention back to Fred. "Could I have a bite of your roll?" she asked.

"What? Sure . . . I guess so. Why don't you go get some lunch?"

"I'm not really that hungry. Besides, Lars will be coming soon. I'd just as soon wait for him."

"Thanks a lot."

"You know what I mean."

"Sure, sure."

Maggie kept one eye on the door and mused over Lars's absence as she conversed with Fred. It was easy to talk to Fred and think about other things at the same time. Fred's questions and answers were mindless and predictable. No matter how vague or irrelevant Maggie's conversation, Fred nodded in agreement. *He's like Andy Bashford*, Maggie thought at one point—*passively agreeable.* She supposed they both had their limits, but she had never pushed either of them far enough to know for sure. She could remember Andy sharing his lunch with her when they were in the first grade—Andy agreeing with everything she said and offering her everything from his dill pickle to his chocolate cupcake.

When Fred had finished his lunch he crumpled his napkin and tossed it onto his plate. "Well, I'm done," he said.

"That's really nice," Maggie replied. She glanced at her watch. It was twelve forty-five. She had a class at one. So did Lars.

Fred lingered at the table a few minutes longer and then excused himself. He had a one o'clock class too. "If I see Lars I'll tell him you're waiting for him," he said as he left.

"Ask him . . . ," Maggie began, then stopped. "Never mind."

"Do you want me to ask him something?"

"No. Never mind. I'll ask him."

"OK. See ya later."

"OK. Bye."

Before long Maggie was the only one left in the cafeteria. Student aides were wiping off the tables and stacking the chairs upside down on the tabletops so they could sweep the floor. Maggie told herself to get up and leave, but her body didn't respond.

Leaving was admitting something.

But finally, when the embarrassment of staying became stronger than the dread of departing, she stood up and walked out of the empty cafeteria. The door clanked shut behind her with a metallic ring and her footsteps echoed along the deserted sidewalk.

It was too late to make her one o'clock class, so Maggie wandered back to her room. She paused anxiously outside the door, afraid she would once again find Linda in tears. But when she pushed the door open she was relieved to find the room vacant. She tossed her handbag onto the bed and plopped down beside it, her chin in her hands. She stared across the room, her eyes dark and hollow.

What boys will excuse in themselves they will

*often not accept in girls—especially not the girl
they choose to marry. . . .*

*God understands, I'm just not so sure he
approves.*

Maggie glanced at her watch. She had another
class at two. Old Testament Survey. She closed
her eyes and tried to imagine herself sitting in
class, calmly taking notes.

*The Abrahamic Covenant: A covenant between
God and Abraham sealed by the rite of circumcision.*

She squeezed her eyes together and clenched
her fists. Once again she tried to picture herself
in class, her legs crossed, her arm resting on the
desk top, her pen poised to take notes.

*"You are to undergo circumcision, and it will
be the sign of the covenant between me and
you. . . . "*

Circumcision. . . . She'd asked about it once in
Sunday school. Her teacher had mumbled something—embarrassed. Lars, Andy, and the other
boys had giggled and whispered.

Next she saw herself jumping up and screaming, scattering her books and papers across the
floor. *That's right!* she screamed, not knowing
what she was saying. She screamed at the teacher
and at the other students about a bloody covenant
between men and God that she could be no part
of. She should have known that a God who sealed
his covenants with a rite like circumcision—
something so . . . so *male*—would not look upon
the sins of a woman in the same light as the sins
of a man. She hurled her angry words at them

and then fell to her knees beside her desk amid her scattered notes, her head thrown back. An anguished moan trailed into a soft wail and then disappeared into silence.

She decided to skip class.

Maggie opened her eyes and stared at the buzzer on the wall. It would ring any minute. No doubt Lars was standing in the lobby ready to press the button. This very moment he was probably rushing across campus, eager to tell her about his argument with Dr. Trimble. Just now he was dialing the telephone. In a moment the telephone in the hall would ring and she would rush to it and he would say, "Maggie, is that you? Maggie, I love you. I love you, Maggie."

But the telephone in the hall didn't ring, and the buzzer on the wall remained silent. Maggie walked to the window and stared across the damp, leaf-littered campus. It was deserted. Everyone was in class, or studying, or . . . or praying.

Maggie walked to her closet and methodically undressed. She stood before the full-length mirror and stared at her naked body. Then she shivered and reached for her robe. She pulled her robe tightly around herself and headed for the shower. The noise of the shower would drown out the silence of the telephone and the steam would surround her, clearing her pores and her mind at the same time.

But when she returned to her room a few minutes later, her face flushed and her hair damp and curly, her mind was as muddled as before. She pulled on an old pair of wool slacks and a baggy sweater. She had been needing a new spiral notebook. This was a good time to go to the bookstore and get it. If Lars called, the phone would ring, ring, ring in the empty hallway. She smiled. Then Lars would have to wait.

But as she stepped into the hall and saw the pay telephone with its metal coin slots and the directions for dialing, she froze. It could ring any moment. What if she heard it ringing when she got to the bottom of the stairs? What if, although she hurried as fast as she could, when she got back to the phone it had quit ringing, and instead of Lars's warm voice, all she heard was the nagging, mocking dial tone? She straightened her shoulders. It wouldn't ring. Lars and God and Dr. Trimble were all off someplace where they didn't have telephones.

She walked briskly down the hall. But when she got to the top of the stairs she stopped and smashed her fist against the rail. Her shoulders sagged. She turned around and slowly walked back to her room, closing the door behind her.

When Linda returned to their room, just before dinner, Maggie was curled up on her bed against the wall. She had yanked the bedspread loose and had pulled it around her shoulders like a shawl. When Linda greeted her, Maggie didn't reply.

"What's the matter?" Linda questioned, "Don't you feel well?"

Maggie shook her head.

"I hope you're not getting the flu," Linda said. "There's a lot of flu going around."

Maggie nodded her head, but still didn't speak.

As Linda began changing her clothes she asked, "Are you coming to dinner?"

Maggie cleared her throat and shook her head. "No," she answered.

Linda paused and looked at Maggie thoughtfully. "Are you sure you're all right? Do you want me to bring you anything?"

"I'm all right."

"Well, OK," Linda said as she grabbed her coat from the bed. "If I see Lars I'll tell him you're not feeling well."

Maggie shook her head violently from side to side. "Don't . . . don't say anything to Lars," she said.

"Maggie . . . well, OK. I'll see you later."

6 MEMORIES

After Linda left, Maggie returned to her silent
vigil. She remained curled up on her bed, her
back to the wall and her knees pressed tightly
against her chest. She pulled the bedspread shawl
more tightly around her shoulders in a pathetic
attempt to ward off the growing reality of double
standards and prejudiced gods. She shivered
inside her cocoon and pulled even more tightly
into herself. The evening shadows crept into the
small rectangular room, but Maggie didn't think
to turn on the light.

*He won't respect you, Maggie. He won't respect
you if you let him talk to you about things like
that.*

Who had said that? One of her girl friends. So
long ago. The summer she and Lars had redis-
covered each other.

As youngsters, Lars and Maggie had been
playmates. She could still see herself running

across the sand toward Lars and Andy Bashford, waving her sand shovel, her braids tossing from side to side. The three of them had played together by the hour, confident and unembarrassed. Then came the bad time—late childhood. For two or three years they had been like strangers. At times like enemies. Lars and Andy, with their army of buddies, had teased Maggie and the other girls until Maggie wanted to scream and claw in frustration.

Then one magic summer everything changed. Lars and Maggie were friends again—but in a new way. On a Sunday school outing Lars wrote her a note asking her to meet him at the old mausoleum. After lunch Maggie had sneaked away from the other picnickers and had arrived at the mausoleum flushed and nervous.

Lars was seated on the ground, his back against one of the old stone pillars. He was poking in the dirt with a broken branch. She had wished she could run up to him as in the old days, confident and unself-conscious, but instead she had paused in the summer grass, uncertain of what to do next.

He must have sensed her presence then, for he looked up and scrambled to his feet. "Hi," he said, tossing the stick into the nearby grass. He took a few steps toward her, spread his hands, and let them fall. He tried for a cocky smile. It turned silly. "You came," he said.

Maggie relaxed. She didn't know how she'd gained it, but somehow she knew she had the upper hand. She lifted her chin and walked toward him. "Yes," she said. She brushed her hand across the gritty surface of an old stone bench. "I haven't been up here for years," she said, walking slowly through the old mausoleum. She studied it all carefully, as if the minute details of each pillar and headstone were tremendously important to her. She was madly trying to think of what to say next. "Well," she said at last, shrugging her shoulders, "I guess it's still just about the same."

"I guess so," Lars said. He jammed his hands into his pants pockets and, nodding his head toward the far end of the monument, said, "Do you know why there's no headstone at that end of the table?"

Maggie knew, of course, but to admit she knew would have brought the fledgling conversation to a close. "No," she said, "why?"

"Because in old man McMillin's dining room that end of the table faced the bay. Mr. McMillin had the chairs arranged so at dinnertime everyone could watch the sunset."

"Really?"

"Yep. Kind of clever, don't you think, being buried according to your place at the dinner table?"

"Well . . . there are different kinds of clever, I suppose."

"You don't like it?"

"I don't know." She furrowed her brow and pondered the burial arrangement. Finally she pinched her lips together and nodded her head ever so slightly. She folded her arms across her chest and tapped her toe in the grass. "I don't know," she repeated. "It's either truly magnificent or very corny."

Lars threw back his head and laughed. Maggie tensed. But then she saw that he was actually amused—he wasn't trying to make her feel silly. His blue eyes sparkled and the skin around the corners of his eyes crinkled pleasantly.

After they had inspected all the names on the headstones and had determined how old each person was when he had died, they sat down on the grass nearby and talked.

As they chatted on the soft, matted grass next to the moss-covered pillars, Maggie and Lars mysteriously regained the easy camaraderie they had known as youngsters.

Lars asked her questions, and when she answered, he listened. The seduction of being heard was irresistible. She told him things girls weren't supposed to admit to boys. For years they had been faced off, one against the other—boys against girls. Now, for some reason, in the soft grass next to the old mausoleum, their differences had been transcended.

The deliciousness of the moment remained with Maggie forever.

"Mag-gie," Rachel had whined, "where were you?"

Maggie's eyes were shiny as she tried to suppress a smile. "Oh, we were just up at the mausoleum," she had said.

"What were you doing?"

"Talking."

"Oh, sure, sure. For two hours you and Lars were up at the mausoleum talking."

"We were."

"What did you talk about?"

"Things."

"What kinds of things?"

"I don't know, just things."

"Are you going together?"

Maggie shrugged her shoulders.

That evening several of the girls spent the night at Maggie's for a slumber party. They gathered on Maggie's bed to hear about her afternoon in the woods.

"Did he kiss you?" Rachel asked breathlessly.

"Is he a good kisser?" the others chimed in.

"No," Maggie said.

"He isn't? He's a bad kisser?" The girls were shocked and disapproving. Their question had been rhetorical. All boys were considered good kissers.

"No, he didn't kiss me," Maggie explained.

"Come on, Maggie," Rachel said. "You were gone for hours. Of course he kissed you!"

"No, he didn't. Besides," Maggie said, a little stiffly, "I'm saving my kisses for my husband."

"Oh, brother," Rachel said. "You'll never even find a husband that way."

Maggie raised her chin stubbornly. "Yes, I will. I'm only going to kiss one boy in my whole life—and that's the boy I marry."

"That's stupid. You've already been kissed."

"I have not."

"You're kidding! You've never been kissed?"

"Never!"

There were whispered exclamations of doubt all around the ragged circle of girls huddled together on Maggie's bed. Shivering in their baby-doll pajamas, they eagerly began questioning each other about the boys they'd kissed. After they had shared all their secrets, including various incidents involving cousins and brothers, Maggie remained the only one who had never been kissed by a boy—ever.

"But you have to have been kissed by Andy," Rachel said. "Andy's kissed everyone." Rachel's voice betrayed some of the awe she felt for her older brother's friendly charm.

"Not me," Maggie said, lifting her chin proudly. "And I'm not going to marry a boy who has kissed other girls."

Rachel heaved a sigh. "Maggie," she said, using her most maternal tone, "you're never going to find a boy who hasn't kissed other girls. They all kiss girls."

"No, they don't," Maggie said quietly. The soft authority in her voice created a hush in the room. But then the girls started taunting her again, insisting it would be impossible to find a boy who had never kissed a girl. Maggie's cheeks flushed. She hesitated, then said, "Lars has never kissed a girl." Her voice carried just a hint of "I-told-you-so."

"How do you know?" asked one of the girls, pronouncing the words in a sing-song manner.

"Because he told me," Maggie replied, imitating her sarcastic tone.

Rachel was aghast. "He told you? You talked to Lars about kissing?"

"You talked about it?" another girl said. "Ooh, I could never talk about kissing to a boy."

"Me either."

Maggie hunched her shoulders forward and

rested her elbows on her knees, pressing her advantage. "That's not all we talked about," she said, her voice full of suggestion.

There were tiny gasps around the circle, and the girls shifted imperceptibly closer to Maggie.

"What else?" Rachel whispered.

"What do you think we talked about?" Maggie countered.

Nobody replied. Finally Rachel said, "You didn't talk about 'it,' did you?"

"What?"

"You know. You didn't, did you?"

"No," Maggie said. "We didn't talk about that."

There were communal sighs of relief and disappointment.

"Well, what then?"

"Well . . . ," Maggie began, leaning forward and making her voice quieter still, "well . . . you know. Hopes and dreams . . . fears."

"He won't respect you, Maggie. He won't respect you if you let him know too much."

Maggie shrugged her shoulders.

Maggie's buzzer interrupted her thoughts. She quickly discarded the bedspread and rushed to buzz back. Twice. "I'll be right down."

She stumbled over her shoes, realized the room was dark, and quickly switched on the light. She paused in front of the mirror, trying to pull her baggy sweater into shape and patting her cheeks to bring back their color. Then she ran through the hall and down the steps.

When she got to the bottom of the stairs she stared about the lobby in confusion. Lars wasn't there. The only person she recognized in the lobby was Fred. He was walking crazily toward her with a white envelope in his hand.

"Lars asked me to give you this," he said.

Maggie stared at the envelope. "Margaret," it said. *Margaret.* She mumbled something to Fred and turned to go up the stairs. When she got to the top she dashed down the hallway and into the restroom. She locked herself in one of the smelly stalls. With trembling fingers she opened the envelope.

The note was brief. Maggie read it again and again, emphasizing first one word and then another, hoping to change the meaning. The color had drained from her cheeks and she leaned against the cold metal wall.

"I cannot see you anymore," the squarish letters said. "I love you more than anything—except my God—but I cannot see you anymore."

7 THE BREAK

Blessings didn't have to be prepared for.

Only disasters.

But Maggie's only preparation had been to tell herself she couldn't bear it. If what Dr. Trimble had said was true, she didn't want to live. All she wanted was to get away—to go somewhere and die. The island was as good a place as any.

Andy Bashford was there to welcome Maggie when she got home. He tried to calm her ragged nerves. She tried to let him.

She didn't see Lars again. He didn't try to contact her, even after she returned home, and she refused to go to him again. It was a sudden, searing break. The swiftness of it should have made it clean.

It didn't.

The marriage of Maggie Hanson and Andrew Bashford was something of a curiosity to the inhabitants of San Juan. The year-rounders on the island had expected Maggie to marry Lars Engles. As children, Lars, Maggie, and Andrew had been inseparable; but Andrew had always been in the background—as easily overlooked as the cap of fog hovering over the cape. They had never expected him to end up with fiery Maggie Hanson. The fact that Lars hadn't come to the wedding caused further speculation. "You have to watch out for them quiet ones," was the usual explanation.

One Saturday morning Maggie slept late. Andrew chided her gently. There were more practical ways to spend a Saturday morning. He had been up for hours, giving the house its monthly inspection. He had carefully jotted down any repairs that needed to be done in the little notebook he carried. His notebook had twelve dividers and was cross-indexed. To appease him, Maggie donned her grimy work clothes. The flower beds next to the house were hopelessly overgrown.

The house belonged to Andrew's parents. His family raised cattle and had lived on the island for three generations. When Andrew asked Maggie to marry him, he hadn't asked whether or not she wanted to spend the rest of her life on San Juan. It seemed an unnecessary question. Maggie had grown up on the island and had not found it confining. She did not find it confining now.

She did not find it anything.

When Maggie began working on the flower beds, Andrew watched her with loving approval.

He walked over to tell her what a nice job she was doing. She thanked him without looking up. Andrew walked away and Maggie continued to grub in the soil. As she was carefully working on the root of a dandelion, trying to dig it out without leaving part of it behind, her fingers touched something hard and gritty. It was an old brick. Maggie brushed the soil from the top of the brick and then noticed that next to it was another and then another.

It was an old brick path hidden by soil and neglect. Maggie quickly abandoned her work in the flower beds and began unearthing the old pathway. She worked quickly, almost wildly. The discovery of the path filled her with an un-explained frenzy. As the morning passed, a chill wind blew in from the bay, pressing her thin shirt close to her body. Her teeth began to chatter, but she didn't seem to notice. She continued her frantic digging among the old clinkers. Andrew saw her shivering in the chilly sea air and suggested she put on a jacket.

"I'm OK," she said.

But it was as if she hadn't heard him.

As she worked on the path, the evidence of the buried past, digging out the hidden bricks, brushing them clean and resetting them in the salty, sandy earth, she rehearsed the fragmented puzzle of her own past. She tried to piece it together in a meaningful pattern.

There were still so many things she didn't under-stand—Lars, his God—their crazy double-stan-dard world. She had walked 'round and 'round the campus that cold November evening trying to reconcile the love of Lars and God with what they had done to her—to their betrayal. She had walked along the leaf-littered campus sidewalks—around the administration building, behind the music building, past the cafeteria with its murky odors, and around the student union building—trying to make sense of things. She was shivering and numb with cold and fear. In desperation she had walked into the lobby of the boys' dorm and pressed Lars's buzzer.

When Lars came down the stairway his hair was disheveled and his eyes were red and watery. He saw Maggie and his lips turned white. He swirled around and started back up the stairway.

"Lars, wait!" she said, hurrying toward the stairwell. Out of the corner of her eye she saw the heads of the boys in the lobby turning in her direction. She didn't care. "Please—wait."

Lars was standing at the top of the stairs, staring down at her, his dark eyes sunk deep in his handsome pale face. He shook his head slowly. "Maggie, please. I can't see you."

"You have to!" she said. She glanced over her shoulder. "Lars, please," she said more quietly. "You owe me that much. Don't you think you owe me an explanation?"

She saw an emotion she couldn't name sweep across his face, but he shook his head. "It won't change anything, Maggie. Nothing you say or I say will change anything."

She leaned forward, her arm against the stair rail. "But, Lars, please. I love you," she said quietly. "I'd do anything for you . . . anything."

Lars lowered his head. "I know," he said. "That's the trouble."

Maggie gasped. Secret dread drained the color from her cheeks. She stared at Lars in disbelief.

"Maggie, I didn't mean . . . wait, Maggie. Wait!"

Lars leaped down the stairs two at a time. But he was too late. Maggie was gone.

Maggie shivered in the cold sea air and continued her frantic uncovering of the old brick path. She had to follow it to the end—uncover it all, expose it to the reality of today. Know the truth.

She should have read his note. At least she could have read Lars's note—the rectangular white envelope with squarish letters. *Margaret.*

But she had been too angry. She had ignored the buzzer as she yanked clothes from the closet and jammed them into the open suitcase on the bed. She had already packed her books in a cardboard box and was trying to decide what to do with her towels and sheets.

Linda had rushed into the room and then stopped and stared around in amazement. Maggie had stripped the bedding from her bed. It was heaped on the floor. Her cosmetics were strewn across the bed beside her suitcase and a tangled pile of shoes prevented the door from opening all the way.

"What in the world are you doing?" Linda wanted to know, glancing behind the door to see why she couldn't get it open. She stared at Maggie, her hands on her hips. "What's going on here?"

"Nothing," Maggie said, snapping shut the

latches on her cosmetic case.

"Right," Linda said. She wended her way across the room, side-stepping the pile of blankets and shoving Maggie's clock radio against the bed with her foot. She studied Maggie in silence for a few moments, then said, "I ran into Lars in the lobby. He asked me to give you this." She extended her hand.

She was holding a white envelope.

Maggie turned in slow motion until she was facing Linda squarely. "Tell Lars," she said slowly and evenly, "that I quit passing notes when I was thirteen."

Linda stared at Maggie. She was still holding the envelope toward her. Maggie's arms were rigid at her sides, her fists clenched tightly. After a moment Linda placed the envelope on Maggie's desk. "Well," she said, "I'll just leave it right here." She patted the envelope three times lightly. "Maybe you'll want to read it later."

Maggie whirled on her. "I'm not going to read it now, I'm not going to read it later, I'm not going to read it ever!" Maggie snatched the envelope from the desk and thrust it back into Linda's hand. "You can just take this back to Lars," she said, her eyes flashing, "and tell him he can keep his little notes and his little God all to himself!"

Andrew again suggested Maggie go get her jacket. When she refused, Andrew got it for her. He brought it to her, insisting that she put it on. "Why don't you stop for today? It's really getting cold," he said.

Maggie shook her head.

God. That was the big trouble. Lars and his God. She had to forget about the God she had known as a child—a God who had smiled down on her with the shining light of his righteousness and love. That God didn't exist. Lars had killed him—maimed him, at least. A dead God was better than a crippled one—a dreadful God distorted by double standards and secret rites. Besides, if God didn't exist then she could be sure no one else loved him either. Or was loved by him. Like Lars.

Maggie zipped her jacket and attacked the hidden bricks with renewed vigor. She had to uncover them all. She didn't want to be startled by any more secret roads leading to peculiar places filled with joy and laughter—the land she had longed for. She wanted to be safe. No surprises. What was it Mr. Engles had said? Something about barnacles.

"They lock themselves on for life."

She had run into him on the beach, shortly after she'd dropped out of college. He had been surprised at seeing her. Confused.

"Why, Margaret," he'd said as he approached, "I almost didn't recognize you. You're out early."

"I wanted to catch low tide."

"Me, too," he said. "But I didn't realize you were a beachcomber."

"Oh . . . I'm not, really. I mean, I like walking along the beach, but I . . . I don't really know how to do it right."

"Do it right?" he said.

"Well, I mean, I'm not an expert like you. I'm probably upsetting the balance of nature or something—putting rocks back upside down and killing millions of little eggs." She lifted her hands helplessly and he smiled.

"Well, I'm not sure the balance of nature is that easily upset," he said. "But, it's true, we probably don't realize our own impact on things." He frowned. Maggie moved slightly, as if inclined to resume her solitary wandering. But Mr. Engles had jammed the driftwood stick he was carrying into the sand next to her foot as if staking a claim. Maggie felt as compelled as the stick to remain still until Mr. Engles indicated it was time for her to move on.

"Lars wrote to say he wouldn't be home for Christmas—he's going to help at some mission down in the slums. He mentioned you had dropped out of school. He didn't say why."

He twisted the stick deeper into the sand, letting his words hang awkwardly in the air. As a hobby, Mr. Engles studied snails—he had that kind of patience. He eyed Maggie calmly.

Maggie shifted uncomfortably. "Well, he knows why," she said quietly. But her words were edged in anger and her anger hung in the air as awkwardly as Mr. Engles's unasked question. He remained quiet and Maggie found new words to fill the silence. "I'm going to get married," she said, tilting her head to one side.

Mr. Engles didn't say anything, but his surprise showed in the tightening of tiny muscles around his eyes.

"Andy Bashford," Maggie added.

"Andrew Bashford, huh?" Mr. Engles shook his head, in wonder rather than disapproval.

Maggie shifted from one foot to the other. "Why should I bother with college when all I'm going to do is get married?"

"All you're going to do?"

"I didn't mean it like that," she said, irritated that he had picked up on that rather than the futility of finishing college. She knelt down and poked at the barnacles on the nearby rock. Mr. Engles knelt down beside her. "Do you know anything about barnacles?" he asked, jabbing at them with his stick.

"They're a nuisance on ship bottoms," Maggie said, summing up her knowledge neatly.

Mr. Engles squinted his eyes and stared at the line in the distance where the ocean met the sky. "In their youth, barnacles are quite the young gadabouts," he said. "They swim around, foot-loose and fancy free, like shrimp and other shellfish. But as they approach adulthood they find a rock or some other hard surface and they glue themselves to it—for life." Mr. Engles glanced up at Maggie. "It's as if security is more important to them than anything else. They build a little fort around themselves and there they stay, the rest of their lives. They're safe, I suppose, but it sounds pretty dull to me. Don't you agree, Margaret?"

Maggie followed Mr. Engles's gaze to the horizon, and then as he rose to his feet she lifted her chin slightly and faced him.

"It sounds rather nice," she said.

8 WEDDING

Maggie worked frantically on the old path for weeks. All the weeds had to be yanked away and the old bricks—some of them clinkers, burned hard and black—had to be lined up neatly and accurately. She wanted to look at them and know they were fixed and still, wedged tightly one against the other.

Since the wedding, Maggie had lived in the safe, predictable world of her endurance. What she feared was the world she longed for. There was no longer any one point at which her life intersected with the world she had dreamed of as a child. Her childish mind had been filled with dreams of a God who loved her and of a man who would take care of her. For as long as she could remember, the man in her dreams had been a grown-up version of Lars Graham Engles and the God who loved her was good.

But in the world in which she lived, Lars had betrayed her and God wasn't good. Instead, she lived in a mundane world stripped of all that was divine and magic.

Andrew had set the wedding date—February 14. He thought getting married on Valentine's Day would be romantic. Maggie hadn't argued with him.

As Maggie had stood at the back of the church in her wedding gown, waiting for her cue, she had checked to make sure the train of her off-white gown wasn't twisted.

Off-white.

Only slightly tainted.

Her mother had been horrified. They had argued about the color of her gown in the spacious wallpapered dressing room at the Bon Marche in Seattle.

"Margaret, people will think you're not a virgin."

Maggie had stared at her mother. "Don't be silly," she'd said.

The ceremony had been short and simple. At the conclusion, Pastor Thomas had said, "I now present to you Mr. and Mrs. Andrew Bashford." Then he had leaned forward and whispered to Andrew, "You may kiss the bride."

Andrew had smiled and carefully lifted Maggie's veil, taking an extra moment to smooth it down so it wasn't standing up awkwardly in back. Then he had leaned forward and kissed Maggie softly on the lips.

"I'm only going to kiss one boy in my whole life—the boy I marry."

". . . But you must have been kissed by Andy—Andy's kissed everyone."

The reception was a cheerful affair with sticky white cake and pink punch. Maggie's mother beamed as her friends and neighbors commented on her beautiful daughter. They assured her it was a lovely wedding. She thanked them with a humble smile, in a way that silently assured them she had done her best, but well. . . .

Andrew's sister, Rachel, came through the reception line and kissed Andrew on the lips. She gave Maggie a warm hug. "I always knew you two were right for each other," she said. "I knew it way back in first grade."

"Really?" Maggie said.

When Lars's parents came through the line, Lars's father gripped Andrew's hand firmly and said, "You take care of that girl, now. She's special." Then Mr. Engles turned from Andrew to Maggie and engulfed her in a warm yet fervent hug. Maggie's eyes burned. Then Mr. Engles looked into Maggie's face and tilted his head to one side, as if still trying to put together the pieces of an ancient puzzle. "You be happy, Maggie girl," he said. His startling blue eyes, so much like Lars's, shined into hers.

Maggie nodded her head.

The photographer motioned toward the reception table. "I think we're supposed to go have some cake and punch so he can take pictures," she said. She took Andrew by the hand and they squeezed their way through the crowd. They placed themselves behind the three-tiered wedding cake. It was still intact. The photographer had instructed Maggie's aunt not to cut the cake until he could get a picture of the bride and groom behind it. The wedding guests were getting impatient.

Maggie cut a piece of the cake with the silver cake server and held it out to Andrew, who opened his mouth wide while the photographer snapped a picture. Then Andrew cut a piece for Maggie and she obediently bit off a corner for the camera. They smiled at each other and clinked together two glasses of pink punch. The camera snapped.

As soon as the pictures were over, Maggie and Andrew went to their respective Sunday school class/dressing rooms to change their clothes. Later when they met outside the door of Maggie's dressing room, Maggie stared at Andrew in dismay. *He's wearing the wrong shirt,* she thought. But when she tried to visualize the right shirt, she couldn't. Andrew was beaming at her, a silly smile splashed across his face.

The ever-present photographer was lingering nearby to take their going-away picture. He was a little impatient with them as he explained where he wanted them to stand. Maggie was wearing a burgundy traveling suit with matching everything. As she smiled into the camera she couldn't get her mind off Andrew's shirt. *Why is he wearing his old shirt? Not even a tie. How is that going to look in the pictures?*

Maggie and Andrew spent their wedding night ten miles from their little house along the shore. They consummated their marriage in a squeaky wooden bed in the Presidential Suite of the DeHaro Hotel.

Maggie had tried to push Lars from her mind, but he had been there all the while, his easy smile and sparkling eyes sprinkling their splendor over the unbearable. After Andrew fell asleep, Maggie lay next to him in the ancient bed engulfed in a sea of loneliness. She wanted to get up and go to the window, to sit by it and look out over the harbor until she felt connected with something. But she was afraid to move. The springs of the bed groaned miserably if she even tried to turn over. She didn't want to wake Andrew. She lay between the clean white sheets of her wedding bed, desolate and lonely. It was as if Lars had reached into the purity of her marriage bed and had spoiled it from without—polluting it through her mind and through the memories of a commitment that had preceded and transcended her marriage vows.

"I will mother your children and will stay with you always, a faithful helpmeet, friend, and lover. I promise."

Maggie continued to pour the wildness of her disappointment into the old brick path. At first Andrew watched Maggie's progress on the path with approval. It was good to see her interested in something. Except for her job at the bank, she had few interests. There was church. But Maggie seemed to attend the worship services without actually participating in them.

Then after a while he began to find Maggie's preoccupation with the path disturbing—unnatural. It seemed to be the only thing that brought her pleasure. Not pleasure exactly—a strange absorption. Even in the winter months she swept it clean of leaves and cleared away the litter of time.

The years passed. Maggie existed. She worked at the bank and lived with Andrew. She went to church and worked in the yard. As she toiled on the old path—ordering and reordering her miniature world—she thought of Lars and of his God.

They were both in Ecuador.

Lars had become a missionary. Saving lost souls.

In the dark hours after midnight one February night, when Maggie and Andrew had been married nearly five years, Maggie awoke as usual, bathed in sweat. It happened nearly every night. She wasn't sure when the nightmares had started. It seemed she'd been having them forever.

Every night she tried to relax. By now she had a regular routine. She'd read about it in a magazine. She moved stealthily from her stomach to her back and closed her eyes, tensing her muscles. Then, one by one, she relaxed them, starting with her toes, then her arms and legs, and gradually the rest of her body. The magazine article had promised it would work, but she could still feel the tension and stiffness across her shoulders and up into her neck. She *had* to relax. She tried pretending her body was a block of cement. Heavy, heavy, sinking into the bed. Even her head. A block of concrete, leaden and dull. But the memory of her nightmare pierced her and she began to tremble. Her cement body crumbled and once again she was bathed in sweat.

Nothing worked.

As she'd done countless nights before, Maggie crept from her bed and sneaked into the bathroom. It was ridiculous. She'd never once forgotten. But she pulled the door of the medicine cabinet open and reached for the little round plastic container of pills. She stared at the last exposed date and shivered. Of course—she'd remembered. She pressed her hand against her breast, trying to quiet her pounding heart. She remembered taking it now—just after brushing her teeth. But someday she'd forget. She knew it.

Sometimes she awoke two or three times in the night, sure that she had not remembered to take her birth control pill.

Andrew didn't understand Maggie's fear. It was the one source of real conflict between them. Andrew was ready to start a family. They could afford it and he had always loved children. Maggie had loved children too, but . . . it was hard to explain. Even to herself. She didn't try to explain it to Andrew. She told Andrew she just wasn't ready to be tied down yet. She needed more time.

But five years was time enough.

The truth was she didn't want children at all—ever. In the still darkness of the early morning, Maggie pondered Andrew's growing obsession with babies and her deepening revulsion. She understood his feelings better than her own.

She remembered how she and Lars had talked and talked about having children. They had imagined what their children would look like and what their names would be. They had planned out the lives of their unconceived children, watching them riding their bikes and graduating from college. Always the children they had envisioned were mixed up versions of themselves—his eyes, her nose, his laugh, her walk. Their imaginary children had been one of their great joys.

But whenever Andrew mentioned children, Maggie's body stiffened and her thoughts became erratic, bouncing about in confusion.

She was too restless to go back to bed. She prowled around the house for more than an hour. For a while she tried to read, but when she couldn't concentrate, she stood in front of the living room window staring toward the invisible, murmuring sea.

The sleepless nights were beginning to take their toll. The nightmare images that awakened Maggie during the deep, dark hours began haunting her in the daytime as well. She was beginning to lose weight and the doctor had crinkled his forehead in a worried frown. "I don't understand it," he said, "it's almost as if your body is trying to shut itself down."

It was getting hard for her to concentrate at work and people were beginning to whisper behind her back. Time and again she failed to balance at the end of the day. Her boss began making excuses to linger near her teller cage at closing time so he could watch her count her cash.

Maggie didn't know how much longer she could stand it. If only the nightmares would stop. Once the nightmares were gone she knew she would be OK.

Finally, shivering with cold, she went back to bed and lay flat on her back, staring into the darkness. She couldn't get enough air into her lungs. She tossed and turned most of the night. Just as she drifted to sleep she saw herself talking to Andrew—carefully explaining something to him, quietly and credibly. Her face was assured and rather sad, as if she were telling him something she knew would be painful, but which, nevertheless, had to be said. Andrew nodded sadly and slowly, without so much as a flick of an eyelash to suggest he didn't believe what she was saying. The picture was fading and Maggie tried to pull it back—so she could hear her words. But she couldn't hear, and before long even the faces disappeared.

Then she and Lars were in the basement of the music building trying to make love. People kept knocking on the door and walking into the room. As soon as one person left another came in. Then the room was filled with little kids, running over the furniture, shouting and screaming. Maggie was holding a baby. But when she looked at it she screamed.

It was a squirrel.

The dream was not always the same. The old man was always there—standing in the background in his flowing white robes, wagging his finger—but the babies were different. Sometimes they were squirrels and sometimes kittens. One time it was a snake. Usually it had Lars's face, but sometimes it had Andrew's. One time she didn't recognize the face, but she knew it was her dead father. Night after night Maggie gave birth to grotesque creatures that filled her with loathing and a certain mad longing.

9 A SCARE

"No, Andrew. It's not necessary. Really, it's nothing. The doctors just want to run some tests. Rachel will be close by and—well, you know Rachel. She'll take wonderful care of me."

Maggie's voice was even and her face was a little sad, as it had been in her dream. But the words were not the same. She had not heard the words of her dream but she knew she was not using them. She didn't need to. It would be enough for her to know.

Maggie did not ordinarily like to be fussed over. But the afternoon she arrived at Rachel's after her stay in the Seattle hospital, she luxuriated in her sister-in-law's tender care. Rachel fussed about, bringing her pillows and glasses of orange juice. "What did that doctor do to you, anyway?" she asked at one point. "You really look drained. How many tests did they run?"

Maggie waved her hand through the air in a vague gesture, suggesting she couldn't begin to count them or in any way explain what the awful doctor had put her through. "I don't know," she said. "You know doctors—they never explain what they're doing."

"You could always ask, you know," Rachel said. "You have a right to know what they're doing. It's your body, for heaven's sake."

"I don't normally perform tubal ligations without the husband's consent," the doctor had said.

"It's my body," Maggie had replied. *"If I don't want to produce babies in my body, whose business is it but my own?"*

The doctor had moved his head from side to side in disapproval. "Your husband has a right to take part in this discussion," he insisted. "Besides, you're very young. You may feel differently in five or ten years. When women turn thirty they often change their minds. The operation is sometimes reversible but I don't like. . . ."

Maggie's lips were drawn together in a tight, angry line when she left his office. She found the counselor at the birth control clinic more helpful. There was a large poster on the wall behind her desk.

ABORTION:
EVERY WOMAN'S CHOICE.

"Many doctors don't like to do tubal ligations without the husband's permission," the counselor said calmly, "but you have the legal right of consent. If you want the operation, you can have it. I can give you the names of some doctors who will be sensitive to your dilemma."

After Maggie left the clinic she picked one of the names at random. When she called him he agreed to perform the operation. He didn't seem concerned about latent maternal instincts.

Maggie slouched back against the cushions on the couch and took a sip of her orange juice. "He seemed to know what he was doing," she said. Her manner suggested tired resignation and a certain unwillingness to discuss it further.

She closed her eyes. The dreams had gotten unbearable—real babies. But dead and stiff, like wooden dolls. And strangely formed, with hands at the elbows and ears in the wrong places—high on the cheekbones. And the same old man was always there in his flowing gown. Maggie would shove the stiff baby bodies at him, but he would shake his head, refusing to take them.

"But I don't want them, I don't want them."
He would turn and walk away.

The next morning Maggie made a point of getting up early and presenting herself fully dressed at the breakfast table. Her knees were shaky and she wanted nothing more than to crawl back into bed. But she smiled her way through three cups of coffee and in weary admiration watched Rachel get Cal off to work, Peter off to preschool, and Annie fed and back down for a nap.

There was more bleeding than she had anticipated. The doctor hadn't told her what to expect.

Later in the morning Rachel had to run some errands. "Annie's asleep in her crib," she said, "do you suppose . . . ?"

Maggie waved her hand through the air. "We'll be fine," she said.

Rachel hesitated. "Well . . . OK. If she wakes up there's a bottle in the refrigerator."

"Great."

After Rachel left, Maggie shuffled back to the room she was sharing with Annie. She peeked in on Annie—sound asleep in her crib, making funny little sucking and sighing sounds—and then turned to her own bed, intending to make it.

So tired.

Instead of straightening it, she plopped down on it.

It had been a gallant gesture—getting dressed and going through the morning routine with Cal, Rachel, and the children. But now she felt drained. If only she could admit how tired she was. But Rachel might become suspicious—was already curious.

"What did those doctors do to you, anyway?"

I feel so weak. Maggie curled up on the squeaky twin bed. She hoped Annie wouldn't wake up until Rachel got home. She drifted in and out of sleep. She had dreams. Bad ones. And when she woke up her teeth ached. She'd been grinding them. The operation was supposed to take care of the dreams.

So tired.

Annie was moving restlessly in her crib. Maggie could hear the tiny, baby-soft fingernails scraping against the crib sheet as Annie's movements became more agitated. At last Annie gave out a tiny baby wail. Maggie let her squall for a while, until she was sure she was awake, not just dreaming. Then she wearily rose to get Annie's bottle from the refrigerator.

She felt dizzy. A spreading patch of red. She stared in horror at the bed. She had been lying in a pool of blood. She slumped against the bed. Annie was screaming and thrashing, her tiny little eyes squeezed tight and her face scrunched into a mass of wrinkles. She threw her tiny fists through the air in erratic movements of helpless frustration. *The blood. What?*

Bottle. In the refrigerator. Shut up. Shut up.

Maggie pulled the blood-stained sheet from the bed and wrapped it between her legs. *Mustn't stain the carpet.* She took the few steps to the doorway and then paused, leaning against the door jamb for support. Then she moved out into the hall, leaving behind a bloody handprint on Annie's doorpost. She staggered to the refrigerator. Annie's screams were loud and shrill, piercing the marrow of Maggie's bones.

Shut up. She took the bottle from the refrigerator and made her way back to the bedroom. Maggie propped the bottle on a pillow and put the nipple in Annie's mouth. The milk was cold— Rachel usually warmed it. Annie sucked on it a few times and then pulled her lips away, screwing up her face and wailing in protest.

Maggie was hanging over the side of the crib, dizzy and weak. "Come on, Annie," she said. "Come on, baby, drink it." She cupped her hands around the bottle, hoping to warm it a little. Then she put the nipple back into Annie's mouth. With her other hand she stroked Annie's damp, baby-soft hair.

After a few moments Annie began sucking strongly on the nipple, swallowing the milk in great gulps. "Good baby," Maggie whispered. When she was sure Annie was all right, she secured the bloody sheet between her legs more tightly and hobbled toward the bed. *Awful.* Blood was everywhere. *Have to clean it up. Not much time. Bath. Clean sheets.*

Somehow she managed to get to the linen closet for fresh sheets. But when she returned to the bedroom, reeling with dizziness, she stared at the sheets and tears filled her eyes. The fresh sheets were already smeared with red. She glanced around the room. It was hopeless. She saw her bloody handprints on the walls, on Annie's crib, even on Annie's bottle. It was no use. *Too tired.*

She slumped onto the bed, and just before closing her eyes she focused on Annie's wide-eyed Raggedy Ann doll on the shelf above the crib. In fragments, not a dream, but in recurring flashes of memory, hanging onto consciousness, she tried to put together a story she'd learned in Sunday school. Something about a stolen doll stuffed with wheat seed. Lied about and buried, sprouting in the spring. A perfect doll-shaped patch of wheat growing in the backyard.

The first thing Rachel noticed when she walked into the house was a blood-stained handprint on the refrigerator door. "My God—Maggie, Annie!"

She hurried to the bedroom. Annie was asleep in her crib. The bottle, nearly empty, had slipped from her lips. There was a little milk mixed in the drool at the corners of her contented mouth. In the same moment Rachel knew Annie was all right she saw Maggie slumped across the bed, pale and wrapped awkwardly in a blood-stained sheet. "Maggie, for heaven's sake, what's wrong? You're bleeding."

"It's OK," Maggie whispered. "Sorry . . . mess."

Rachel helped Maggie into bed and then hurried to the bathroom for some towels. She brought a cold, damp washcloth for her forehead.

"Now, I'm going to go call the doctor," she said with forced calmness. "You just lie there quietly until I get back."

Maggie tried to raise her head from the pillow. "No, no, don't call the doctor. Please, don't. . . ."

Rachel was already in the other room.

When Rachel returned to the nursery, she was pale and tight lipped. She checked the towels to see if the bleeding had stopped, which it had. When she spoke, her voice was quiet and even. Her eyes didn't meet Maggie's. "I think you'll be OK," she said. "He said to bring you in if we couldn't get it stopped."

Maggie followed Rachel around the room with her eyes. Rachel continued to fuss about, changing the bed and bringing in a wash basin to give Maggie a sponge bath. Still she didn't look at Maggie. Her face was set in anger and revulsion.

Finally, when Maggie could no longer stand it, she said, "Rachel . . . did . . . did the doctor say anything else?"

Rachel turned to her then. Her eyes blazed into those of her sister-in-law.

Rachel and Maggie had been friends long before they had become sisters-in-law. As young girls they had understood each other's fiery natures—personalities that flared at the commonplace and rebelled against the restrictions of girlhood. But while Rachel's disposition had mellowed into a glowing flame of devotion, warming her husband, children, and friends, Maggie still carried within her the fiery coals of her youth—embers ready to roar into flames.

Even as Rachel, white lipped and angry, stared at Maggie, she was warmed by the memory of their shared childhood—of all the burning secrets they had shared. She slumped on the bed close to Maggie's feet. "Maggie, how could you?" she whispered. She shook her head. "You did this behind Andy's back? He would never—he wants children so badly." She continued to shake her head. "How could you?"

Maggie stared at Rachel in silence. She had not been prepared for this. She had not planned for Rachel to discover that she had had her tubes tied. And she was not prepared for Rachel's shock.

But Rachel didn't know about the dreams. That was why she was so horrified. If she knew about the dreams she would understand. Sleepless nights and deformed babies. The words of the angry prophet wagging his finger in her face. *"Because of this the child will die."* She couldn't explain it, though. Not to Rachel, not to anyone. She'd tried to make it clear to the doctor. He had just brushed her words aside. "Fine, fine," he'd said. "No need to go into all of that."

"I . . . I had to," Maggie stammered. "You don't understand. Your children are healthy. But what if . . . what if they weren't? What if they were deformed and it were your fault? What if . . . ?"

"Deformed? What are you talking about?"

Maggie put her hands to her face and shook her head from side to side. "I don't know. I don't really know. But I've had these awful dreams and. . . ." Maggie stopped speaking. She stared at Rachel, her eyes standing out, dark and terrified against the pallor of her cheeks. "I don't know." She shook her head. "I don't know!"

Rachel had no idea what Maggie was trying to say. And she didn't have a shred of sympathy for what she'd done; but she could read the fear in her dark, hollow eyes. The doctor had told her Maggie needed rest. Rachel's eyes softened. "Never mind, Maggie. We don't have to talk about it. The doctor said that as long as the bleeding stops you'll be OK. You just need lots of rest." Rachel smoothed Maggie's blankets and fluffed the pillow. Then she stroked her fingers through Maggie's damp hair. She sighed deeply. "You really frightened me," she said. "All that blood!" She shook her head from side to side.

"I'm sorry, Rachel. I didn't mean to drag you into this. But you won't. . . ." She lifted herself away from the pillows. Her body felt heavy and weak. ". . . You won't tell Andrew, will you? Andrew mustn't know." She shook her head. "He mustn't. He would never understand."

Rachel stared at her for a moment. "I don't understand either," she said, anger returning to her voice, "but that's between you and Andy."

Maggie relaxed against the pillows and closed her eyes. Rachel walked to the window and pulled the drapes. "Now you get some sleep," she said. She put her hand on her hip. "Are you sure you're going to be all right? I mean, I don't want to just leave you here in pain."

Maggie opened her eyes and smiled. "I'll be all right," she said. Then she closed her eyelids and snuggled her head deeper into the pillow. Soon she was fast asleep.

When she dreamed it was of the old prophet kneeling on the ground, carefully tending a small, doll-shaped patch of wheat.

10 THE RUINS

Andrew had missed her.

He was waiting at the dock for her when she returned from Seattle to the island. For the next several days he bustled around the house, attentive and thoughtful. When he asked about the tests, Maggie told him they had been nothing—not painful. Inconclusive. It didn't look good for having children, but time would tell. She found it easy to befuddle him with medical terms. She mentioned endometriosis and leiomyoma. And she spoke vaguely of hormonal imbalances. He didn't persist. Andrew had a natural aversion to words he didn't know how to spell. He suggested she see another doctor, but Maggie brushed his suggestion aside.

If Andrew was especially thoughtful and attentive after Maggie's stay in Seattle, Maggie herself was surprisingly solicitous. For some reason the mere sight of Andrew aroused her sympathy. Perhaps it was the overflow of Rachel's compassion—residual pity. Saturday morning she suggested they pack a lunch and go for a picnic. Coming from Maggie, it was an unusual idea. Andrew stared at her with startled pleasure.

"Really?"

"Sure," she said. "Why not? Where would you like to go?"

"You're sure you're up to it?" When Maggie nodded, Andrew slipped his arm around her waist. "You know what would be fun?"

"What?"

He shook his head. "It's dumb. You'll laugh at me."

"Don't be silly, I won't laugh at you."

"Well . . . how about going up to the old mausoleum? I've never been up there."

Maggie burst into laughter. "What?" she said. "You've never been to the mausoleum? Andrew, your family has lived on the island for a hundred years. The mausoleum is a landmark. People come from all over to see it! You've never been up there?"

"You laughed," he said.

"I'm sorry. It's just that I can hardly believe that."

He shook his head. "I know. It's ridiculous. I've just never gotten around to it."

Maggie pinched her lower lip between her fingers thoughtfully. "Well, that would be fun. I can be your tour guide. I know all about it."

Andrew pulled her body close to his. "I missed you," he said.

"I know," she replied.

She would not lie.

The sun was high in the sky when they arrived at the old mausoleum. As she eyed the crumbling stone pillars, she could almost see Lars, as he'd been that summer day so long ago, waiting for her with his back against a pillar, writing in the dirt with a dead branch.

Maggie was ahead of Andrew. She hurried up the old stone steps. "Step this way, folks," she said. "You don't want to miss the legend of the McMillin Mausoleum." She cleared her throat and let her right hand rest lightly on one of the gray stone chairs. "Mr. McMillin had the chairs at the dining room table arranged so that everyone had a view of the sunset," she said. "Then he had their burial plots arranged the same way. That's why there's no stone at that end of the table. Pretty clever, don't you think—being buried according to your place at the dinner table?"

Andrew shrugged his shoulders. "I don't know," he said. "I think it's kind of corny."

Maggie stared at him, then lifted her chin slightly. "Well, I don't," she said. "I think it's magnificent." She gave her head a tiny toss.

Andrew stared at her. A coolness crept into his eyes. "No, you don't," he said. "You think it's corny too."

Maggie stared at him. "Why do you say that?"

"Lars told me."

"Lars told you?"

"He told me about your afternoon up here—how you couldn't decide whether the mausoleum was magnificent or corny. He thought that was really funny." Andrew sat down on one of the stone chairs and stared at the towering pillars. "I was jealous," he said. "I've always wanted to bring you here myself."

Maggie sat down in the stone chair across the table from him. She couldn't think of anything to say. She wanted to say something kind, reassuring. But she couldn't. The air around the old mausoleum was inhabited with spirits of long ago—the seductive spirits which had sucked her and Lars into a delicious intimacy and now rendered Maggie speechless.

"You know where else I've never been?" Andrew said suddenly.

"Where?"

"The ruins."

"The ruins," Maggie murmured. "I've never been there either. My mother always told me not to go down there. There's a warning against trespassing."

"I know. Even Lars was afraid to go down there."

A place where Lars had never been.

It was posted against trespassers, but Maggie and Andrew ignored the signs. "Watch out for that barbed wire," Andrew said.

"Do you think they have an alarm system— dogs, maybe?"

Andrew laughed. "No. They just don't want kids messing around—getting hurt. They could be sued, I suppose."

"Um."

As they approached the old ruins, Maggie grew

quiet. She hung back a little. Something about the old place, the crumbled stone walls overgrown with vines and weeds, reminded her of her brick path. The mystery of the past gnawed at her insides, making them feel raw and aching.

Maybe not. Maybe the rawness was just her incision, not quite healed.

Andrew was immediately engrossed in the remains of the old mansion. He walked from one end to the other, pacing off the distance, trying to figure out the original layout. Finally he paused at one end and gazed out toward the bay—although one could no longer see it from there, the trees had grown so tall. "This must have been the kitchen," he called to Maggie. "Don't you think?"

Maggie climbed over the rubble until she was by his side. She gazed at the vine-covered boulders. "Could be," she said.

Andrew was quiet for a moment. "Didn't McMillin build this house for his son?"

Maggie nodded. "I think so."

Then he said, "His family must have been very important to him."

"I suppose so."

Andrew was thoughtful. "All that business about the chairs at the dinner table—making sure everybody had a view of the sunset. A lot of fathers wouldn't have been that thoughtful." He shrugged his shoulders. "I don't know. Maybe I wouldn't be such a great dad." He waved his arm through the air. "I'd never think of anything like that."

"My father would have," she said. Her tone was

even, her words clipped. She shrugged her shoulders. "But I'm not sure that's what's important."

Andrew stared at her. "I didn't think you could even remember your father."

"Oh, I remember a few things . . . I think."

"You think?"

Maggie sat down on one of the old crumbly stones and pressed the side of her hand against her lips. "I've never been sure," she said. "I . . . I might have dreamed it." She stood up and moved restlessly among the old ruins. She stopped and tapped her closed fist lightly against a broken block of concrete. Her eyebrows were drawn together and her cheeks were pale. She turned to face Andrew.

"But the hurt was real," she said. "I know I didn't dream the anger." She stepped closer to Andrew and then turned her back to him, staring at the view-obscuring trees. "I woke up in the middle of the night," she said. "My grandmother and mother were arguing. When I walked into the living room they stared at me with their mouths open. My father was slumped on the couch—all white and limp. Grandma wanted to take him to the hospital—they were arguing whether or not it was a good idea to move him. They hadn't intended for me to wake up." Maggie spoke quietly into the distance. " 'It's all right, Margaret, it's all right. Daddy will be all right.' " They pulled Daddy to his feet and helped him to the door. I ran after them, pulling on his leg. 'Don't leave me! Don't leave me. Promise me you won't leave me!' "

Maggie stopped. She could hear her child voice

echoing among the old stone ruins. "Mother screamed at me to leave him alone." Maggie touched her hands to her cheeks. "She slapped me across the face. But Daddy raised his hand and motioned toward me. When I got next to him he opened his eyes—tiny slits. 'Don't worry, Maggie,' he whispered. 'I'll be back, I promise. I'll come back.'"

Maggie folded her arms across her chest and moved a few steps away. She shook her head from side to side. "He didn't come back."

"He . . ." Andrew hesitated, ". . . that's when he died?"

Maggie shrugged. "He must have died at the hospital. I don't remember him after that."

"Don't you remember the funeral or anything?"

"I didn't go. Grandma thought it would be too hard on me. Mother argued with her but . . . well, I guess Grandma won again. . . . Grandma usually won."

Maggie resumed her restless pacing—back and forth, back and forth—across the rubble. The muscles of her face were pulled tight across her cheeks and her lips were drawn in a thin line. "He promised," she murmured.

Andrew stared at her. "Maggie, surely you don't blame your. . . ."

Maggie whirled on him. Her eyes were shining and red. "He promised, Andrew. He promised!"

"But, Maggie. . . ."

She shook her head from side to side. "He shouldn't have made a promise he couldn't keep," she said, continuing to shake her head. "People shouldn't make promises they can't keep."

"Sometimes they don't know they can't keep them."

She shook her head fiercely. "Then they shouldn't make them."

11 TRICKED

Another five years passed.

Maggie continued her work at the bank and Andrew slowly took on more of his family's cattle business. They had been married nearly a decade. Occasionally Andrew still mentioned wanting a family, but because it seemed to upset Maggie, he usually dropped the subject.

Lars had come home once on furlough. But he had spent only a few days on the island. He hadn't called on Maggie and Andrew. Maggie hadn't seen him since their encounter on the stairway in the boys' dormitory ten years earlier.

But not a day went by that she didn't think of him.

On Maggie's thirtieth birthday she carried her cash box to her teller window and found several birthday cards waiting for her. She took a moment to open the cards before putting her cash into the drawer. She called out thank yous to those who were close by, and she passed the cards around, letting her co-workers purr over the sentimental greetings and chuckle over the humorous ones— "At your age nothing is impossible—a little silly, perhaps, but not impossible!"

After reading the last card and allowing it to be passed around so others could enjoy it, she put her cash in her drawer and took care of the other early morning banking rituals. By the time the bank opened, she had her teller's cage neatly in order and was prepared to smile her teller's smile.

About halfway through the morning, Mr. Engles came into the bank. He did not come in too often, not daily or weekly like many of her customers, but when he was in the bank he always stopped at Maggie's window.

"Well, Maggie," he said, "how's the birthday girl?"

She folded her arms on the counter and squinted at him quizzically. "How did you re-member it was my birthday?" she asked. Then she laughed, embarrassed. "Oh, the cards." They were standing up around her cage.

Mr. Engles glanced at the cards. "Oh, my . . . you really are celebrating, aren't you? I didn't notice your cards."

Maggie stared at him. "Then how did you know?"

"Lars reminded us."

Maggie felt the color drain from her cheeks. "Lars?" she said, forcing a smile onto her lips. "Lars reminded you?"

"We got a letter from him last week. He said, 'By

the way, the twenty-seventh is Maggie's birthday—wish her a happy birthday for me.' " Mr. Engles let his arm fall through the air in a helpless manner. "So . . . happy birthday."

Maggie became very still. "Thank you," she said. Now her cheeks felt hot. She was flushed and confused. Lars remembered her birthday? After all these years? She remembered his, of course, she *always* remembered his. But . . . he wrote about it—to his parents? Didn't they find that strange? Had he written about her before? Asked about her? Mr. Engles had never said anything. *Relax.*

"How is Lars?" Maggie asked. As she spoke she pulled Mr. Engles's deposit across the counter toward herself. She had regained her casual teller voice. She counted the cash quickly and checked her total against the figure he'd entered on the deposit slip.

"He's OK . . . I guess."

Maggie glanced up.

"I think . . . I think maybe he's been sick. He doesn't come right out and say so, but. . . . Well, he's hinted that he might be home on furlough earlier than he expected and . . . well, Mother says it doesn't sound like he's going out into the remote tribes as much—spends more time at the main base. I wouldn't have noticed that myself. I'm not so good at reading between the lines—but you know how mothers are. Anyway. . . ." He shrugged his shoulders. "It would be nice if he could come home early. We hardly got to see him on his last furlough—he was doing deputation work all the time."

"I . . . I know. I didn't get to see him at all."

Mr. Engles scrunched his shoulders together and fastened his eyes on the countertop. "He's had malaria, you know. He's had it a couple of times."

"But that was years ago, wasn't it? I remember you saying something about it a long time ago."

"Yes, it was at least three years ago." He shook his head from side to side. "But that malaria's funny stuff. Seems like you never quite get rid of it. It comes back again and again."

Maggie's mind seemed to be somewhere else. "Did . . . did he ever get married?" she asked.

"Nope." Mr. Engles said, "never did. But he doesn't run across too many available women out there in the bush, you know. He mentions a young widow once in a while. Her husband was killed in a plane crash—missionary pilot."

Maggie straightened her back. "Well, I'm sure it's nothing for you to worry about—the malaria. He'll be fine—he's tough."

Mr. Engles lifted his head. "I'm not sure he's as tough as you think he is," he said. He picked up his deposit. "Well, did I count the money right this time?"

"Yes." Maggie said. "You always do."

Mr. Engles straightened his shoulders. "Well, I guess I'm all right then. As long as I can still count money, I'm OK." He started to walk away. Suddenly he turned around and walked back to Maggie's window. "Oh, one more thing. Come to think about it, Lars's letter was a little strange— maybe Mother's right. He said. . . ." Mr. Engles waved his hand through the air. "Oh, never mind.

It doesn't even make sense. I think the boy's suffering from fever."

Maggie leaned forward. "No, what? What did he say?"

"Oh, something about a verse in the Bible— about withering grass—and then some mumbo-jumbo about a grass ring. I don't know. He has his mother all upset trying to figure out what he's talking about. She's been studying her concordance, trying to find all the verses about rings and grass. She's driving herself nuts. I guess I'm going to have to write that boy and straighten him out. He's not the only one who's been sick, you know. His mother hasn't been well either. He'll drive her to her grave with his senseless letters. I'll have to write to that boy myself." Mr. Engles shook his head from side to side as if he intended to go right home and do just that.

"The grass withereth." Grass ring. Maggie shook her head to clear away the faint buzzing in her ears. She cleared her throat. "Mrs. Engles has been sick?" she asked, her voice betraying little more emotion than that of suitable concern.

"Oh, it's probably nothing," he said. "Just a little trouble breathing. Well, I guess I'd better get going. Happy birthday, girl. Say hello to your mother when you see her. And Andrew. Remind him what a lucky guy he is."

"I'll do that," she said.

As Maggie expected, there was a surprise party for her at lunch. There was a cake that said, "Happy 30th." And there were more cards. There was even a small flower arrangement from the bookkeeper.

After lunch Maggie returned to her window and set the vase of flowers on the counter where both she and her customers could enjoy it. She added the new cards to those already standing around her teller's cage.

She had no sooner arranged everything to her satisfaction than she glanced up to see a stranger standing just inside the door. He was purposefully eyeing the row of tellers. Probably a tourist. She felt the tiniest tightening of her stomach muscles. Tourists had a way of finding themselves short on cash. They periodically came into the bank expecting the tellers to cheerfully cash their out-of-state checks drawn on unheard-of banks. Sometimes they created scenes—"What do you mean you can't cash my check? This is a bank, isn't it? What's a bank for, anyway?"

Maggie hated scenes.

But when the stranger approached her window, she was relieved to see him take a twenty-dollar bill from his wallet. Change. He just wanted change. He smiled broadly.

"I'd like one ten and ten ones," he said, waving the twenty-dollar bill through the air in an expansive movement. He seemed agitated in a friendly sort of way, as if he had more energy than he knew what to do with.

"One ten, ten ones," Maggie repeated automatically. She reached into her cash drawer and counted out the money. Then she held the bills in her right hand, preparing to count them out to her bouncing customer.

"What's the celebration here?" he inquired. He was inspecting her flowers and trying to read the inscriptions on her birthday cards. "Wow. It must be your birthday."

"Yes, it is," Maggie said, smiling, using her cheerful teller voice.

"Now ain't that somethin'," he said, leaning his elbows on the counter. "Ain't that just somethin'."

He had reddish brown hair and a ruddy complexion. He shook his head from side to side in amazement. Then he began to shift around from foot to foot as if trying to control some inner excitement. "Just like my grandkids'," he said. "Your birthday's the same as my grandkids'."

"Really?" Maggie said. "Kids? More than one?"

"Twins!" he said. He glanced at his watch and then back at Maggie with a broad grin. "They're about four hours old by now."

Maggie's eyes grew large. "You're kidding!" She leaned forward on the counter, the ten-dollar bill and the ten ones still in her hand. "Girls or boys?"

"Girls—two girls. The thing is," the man said, leaning forward confidentially, "our daughter is letting my wife and me name them. My wife, she's got her name all picked out already." He leaned back a bit and glanced at Maggie's name plate.

"What?" Maggie said.

"Melanie," he said. "I have to think of a name that goes nice with Melanie.

Maggie drew her eyebrows together and rested her chin on her hands. "Melanie . . . Melanie," she said. "How about Melissa?"

He shook his head. "No, no, can't stand Melissa." He brightened as if he'd had a sudden inspiration. "What's your name?"

"Maggie," she replied.

"Maggie. That short for Margaret?"

Maggie nodded. "But most people call me Maggie."

"Maggie and Melanie," he said. He tried out the names several times under his breath. "I like that—Maggie and Melanie. That sounds good. I think I'll just name my granddaughter after you! What do you think of that?"

Maggie was surprised by a rush of warmth. She imagined a tiny red-haired baby named Maggie. It made her feel tender and nurturing—protective. "Well . . . really, I hardly know what to say. That would be nice." She wanted to say more—keep him there—savor vicarious motherhood a little longer. But he was already backing away from the counter. He almost bumped into the lady standing in line behind him.

"Oh, excuse me," he said. "I'm sorry, I don't even know what I'm. . . ."

"Oh, wait a minute," Maggie called after him. "I didn't give you your money . . . I got so busy talking. . . ."

The man stumbled back to the counter. "I can't believe it," he said. "I'm just a wreck. I'd have walked right out of here without it."

Maggie counted out the money to him and he stumbled away from the counter.

"Kiss the baby for me," she called after him.

"I will, I will," he said.

After he left the window Maggie glanced around herself in confusion. "Now what did I do with that twenty-dollar bill he gave me?" she muttered. She opened her cash drawer and stared at the stack of twenties as if she might somehow recognize the one he had given her.

There was a lady standing at her window. Maggie hated to keep her waiting, but she felt disoriented. "I must have put it in the drawer," she said. "But I don't usually do that before I give out the change." She looked at the woman at her window. "What did I do with it?" she asked stupidly.

"I don't know," the woman replied.

Maggie shrugged her shoulders and smiled. "Well, I must have put it in the drawer." She pulled the woman's deposit toward herself. "He's naming his granddaughter after me," she said. "Can you imagine that? I don't think I've ever had anyone named after me."

"That's nice," the woman said.

Maggie glanced at the floor, backing up a bit so she could see underneath the counter. Not there.

When Maggie got home from work that afternoon, she put a meat loaf in the oven and then changed into her jeans and sweatshirt. She had an hour or so to work on the brick path before Andrew got home.

She had planted ivy along one side of the path and it had crept pleasantly onto the bricks. Maggie had to keep trimming it back, but it was worth it. The creeping ivy, however, did make the path seem a little narrow. So she had begun collecting used bricks.

Little by little she was widening the path—all the way down to the beach. It took lots and lots of time. But Maggie didn't mind. She had continued to work sporadically on the path ever since the day she had first discovered it. Sometimes she would neglect it for months; then suddenly, for no apparent reason, she would seem obsessed by it, working into the night until it was too dark to see. She had to keep it in order—under control.

One time Andrew had chided her for spending so much time on the path. "Honestly, Margaret, I don't understand what it is about that path. You let the rest of the yard go to pot. You really could divide up your time a little more evenly."

That next evening when Maggie had come into the yard, she found Andrew spraying weed killer between the bricks and along the edge of the path.

"What are you doing?" she had screamed. "Stop it!"

"Wha—?" Andrew had said, startled. "I'm just trying to get rid of these weeds so you won't have to spend so much time keeping the path clear."

"No," Maggie said. She shook her head. "I don't want you to do that."

"Why not?"

"I don't know," she said. "It . . . just . . . it might kill the ivy."

"I'm being very careful. I'm not getting any on the ivy."

"Well, I still don't want you to." She waved her hand through the air aimlessly. "Please. Don't."

Andrew's shoulders dropped and he shifted his weight from one foot to the other, twisting his fingers awkwardly through the handle of the spray can. "I was just trying to help," he said. "It takes so much of your time. I thought maybe we could work on the path together."

Maggie stared at him. *Work on it together?* It

seemed one of the strangest suggestions she'd ever heard.

"I don't mind," she'd said. "I'd just as soon do it myself."

The crunch of gravel in the driveway brought Maggie back to the present. She brushed her soiled hands against her thighs and leaned back to view her work. As usual, she had lost track of time. She was just putting her gardening tools away when Andrew walked around the corner of the house. He looked from Maggie to the brick path and back to Maggie again. "Didn't balance, huh?"

Maggie tossed her spade into the basket and placed her hands on her hips. "How did you know?"

"Psychic."

When Maggie continued to stare at him, not accepting his answer, he said, "You always work on your path when you don't balance."

Her eyes widened in surprise. "I do?" she said.

"Yep. You do."

Maggie studied her husband a moment, processing this new information. Strange. Andrew knew things about her she didn't know about herself. He had been quietly watching her, piecing together the fragments of her personality. What else did he know? *You always work on your path when you don't balance.* Maybe that was all.

After dinner Maggie and Andrew drove to her mother's. Mrs. Hanson had fixed a cake and Andrew had a card and gift for her—a blouse. It wasn't her color.

Maggie told Andrew and her mother about the

man who was going to name his granddaughter after her. "He was so excited," she said. "You wouldn't have believed it. In fact, he was so excited he almost bumped into the lady behind him."

Andrew and Mrs. Hanson laughed at the story about the excited grandfather, but their laughter was halfhearted. Mrs. Hanson always suffered acutely at the mention of grandchildren. She was giving up hope of ever having any. And even talking about other people's babies was painful to Andrew. He still wanted children badly. He couldn't understand Maggie's indifference. She wouldn't even talk about it anymore.

"He almost left without his money," Maggie was saying. "I had to call him back to the window to give him his change." She shook her head from side to side. "He was really a character. He came in flashing that twenty-dollar bill in front of...."

Suddenly Maggie stopped talking and drew her eyebrows together. She was silent for a moment. Then she said, "You know . . . I don't remember seeing that twenty again." She thumped her elbows on the table and rested her chin on her hands. Her face wore a thoughtful scowl. "You don't suppose he—I was twenty dollars short tonight!"

Andrew and her mother had some vague notion of what she was talking about. They listened as she rambled on, talking more to herself than to them. "I didn't make the connection before, but I'll bet he . . . he was so funny. He kept me distracted and then he . . . that flyer we got a while back . . . small-time swindlers. . . ."

She could see him standing there, flashing the twenty-dollar bill. She had turned to her cash drawer, then faced him. *One ten and ten ones. Granddaughter. "Name mine after you." Flush of warmth.*

"He tricked me," she muttered. "Of course. Waving the twenty in my face—getting me all excited about his twins. He was so good I even called him back to the window to give him the money he was cheating me out of!" She slammed her fist against the top of the table.

Tiny lines formed across Maggie's forehead. She began tapping her fingernails rhythmically on the tabletop, shaking her head slowly from side to side. "His daughter didn't have twins," she said. "He was making all that up." Her face was a mixture of anger and sadness. "I thought I was helping him name his grandchild. I thought there was going to be a little baby named Maggie—after me." Suddenly and unexpectedly Maggie's eyes filled with tears.

There wasn't any little Maggie.

There wasn't even a baby.

Maggie got up abruptly and dashed into the bathroom.

12 LOST PIECES

That night Maggie dreamed of Lars. He was lying on the old dusty couch in the basement of the music building. His eyes were hollow—his face gray. The walls of the room were green, and they slowly changed into trees—a jungle. On his arm was a miniature monster with long, spindly legs and a fragile, furry body. Then there were hundreds of them—biting people, sucking their blood. Mosquitoes. Malaria.

Maggie was afraid the nightmares were back. But if she continued to have bad dreams after that, she couldn't remember them. Perhaps they'd gone underground. Sometimes in the mornings her teeth hurt. A bad sign.

The summer of Maggie's thirtieth birthday was hot and dry. Bad for wrinkles, but good for a lot of other things. The tourist trade was up. And the wild blackberries along the road were the plumpest ever. When the breeze was right, she could smell their sweetness all the way up at the house. She decided to get some before they got too ripe.

The blackberry vines were a hopeless tangle. They covered the entire hillside and grew high above Maggie's head. All the plump, heavy berries seemed to be at the top, out of her reach. Previous pickers had faced the same dilemma. Half hidden in the tangled vines were old boards and parts of a broken ladder. Maggie found a long plank and pulled it out of the vines. Groaning with effort, she lifted the board into the air and let it fall. She stepped onto the end of the plank and jumped on it lightly, forcing the opposite end into the briars until it was steady enough for her to use as a ramp.

As she stepped forward she peered into the dark, mysterious world behind the briars. As children, she and Lars had burrowed a little hideaway deep in the brambles. They had huddled in their fort on lazy summer afternoons, plotting pointless deceptions.

"Lars. Maggie. Where are you?" Andrew had called. "Lars?"

They had snickered together in the safety of their fort.

"Shh," Maggie had said.

"We'd better answer," Lars had whispered back.

"No, see if he can find us."

Maggie sighed. If only she could still create a sanctuary for herself inside the briar patch—like Br'er Rabbit. But it was no longer fun. Now the tangled threads of her life were closing in on her, choking out light and hope. She was sinking into the blackness behind the blackberry vines—the blackness of all the evils that had trapped her—deceived her.

Maggie winced. She had reached too far. A row of thorns scraped along her arm. She stared at the little pinpricks of blood. "Blast it," she whispered. She picked a few more handfuls, then stood back from the vines, her hands on her hips, trying to find a more favorable spot to pick.

As her eyes wandered across the hillside of tangled vines, she noticed movement in the distance on the roadway. It was an old man shuffling along the dusty road—walking slowly, easily, absorbing his surroundings. In one hand he was carrying a shiny tin pail. As he swung it back and forth, it caught the bright July sun and sent shafts of startling white light across the countryside and into Maggie's eyes. It was a moment before Maggie realized it was Mr. Engles. She raised her hand to wave at him, but the glaring light from his pail blinded her and she could not see if he recognized her. But a few moments later she saw him wave. "Hello, Maggie girl," he called.

"Hello," she replied when he got closer. "Are you going to steal some of my berries?"

He laughed. "Your berries, huh? What makes you think they're yours?"

"I was here first," she said.

They joked and teased each other for several minutes. Finally Maggie agreed to let him pick some of her berries. Maggie resumed her picking and Mr. Engles found a spot nearby where the berries were closer to the ground. They worked side by side, lazily picking the plump berries and chatting quietly when they felt like it. Their hands became stained with the dark berry juice. And because they could not resist occasionally popping the ripe berries into their mouths, their teeth became discolored—shaded ever so slightly to an eerie shade of gray.

"Is Mrs. Engles going to make a pie?" Maggie asked.

"What? No. Marion hasn't been feeling well. I thought some berries and cream might cheer her up."

"That's right. You mentioned that she'd been sick. She's not getting better?"

Mr. Engles's face became drawn, all the little lines of age straining downward. "No . . . she doesn't seem to be getting any better. She has trouble breathing, high blood pressure. . . ." His words drifted into nothingness.

Maggie studied his tired face. Then she moved closer to him and set her plastic pail on the ground. She plopped onto the ground close to his feet and looked up at him. "You're worried, aren't you?"

Mr. Engles stooped to reach some berries close to the ground. With both hands he quietly removed the berries from the vine and dropped them into his shiny tin pail. Then he sighed and lowered himself onto the grass next to Maggie. He stared into the densely tangled blackberry vines, then drew his eyebrows together in a puzzled frown.

"You know, I always thought by the time we got

this age, death would seem natural." He shook his head. "But it seems as outragious as ever—a perversion. It's no easier to comprehend now than it's ever been." He cleared his throat and lifted his chin, staring into the cloudless sky. "We have eternal life, of course, we know that. But . . . well, this life is all we're familiar with. Death seems so . . . so final . . . so lonely."

Maggie's face clouded. She felt angry. At Mr. Engles? No. At God. Everything was so botched. Lost pieces. Messed up lives. Ugly deaths. Surely God could have arranged things more tidily. It all seemed so . . . so unnecessary. "I just don't understand," she said quietly, more to herself than to Mr. Engles.

"What—death?"

Maggie picked up a dirt clod and tossed it onto the roadway. "Any of it. Death. Suffering." She clenched her teeth. "Hate. Why would God allow things like that? I just can't worship a God like that."

Mr. Engles's body became very still. He sat as if in the presence of a tiny bird he didn't want to frighten away. "Like what?" he asked quietly.

"A bad God. An evil God. Nobody should worship a God who allows death and suffering—injustice. It's not right." She aimlessly tossed a few more tiny dirt clods onto the road. "I mean, if God isn't fair, aren't we justified in not worshiping him?"

Mr. Engles's face was solemn as he looked into Maggie's frightened, defiant eyes. He loved Maggie like a daughter—had always thought she would be someday. He frowned. "You think you're more righteous than God?" he asked.

Maggie shrugged.

Mr. Engles stared into the blackberry bramble. He squinted his eyes as if trying to understand the mysterious tangle of vines and thorns. "I don't know, Maggie," he said. "God is worthy of worship because he is all good." He studied Maggie's face. "Do you worship God at all?"

She shook her head.

"You're angry at him—because you think he isn't fair?"

"Among other things."

Mr. Engles studied the berries in his bucket. He picked out some stray pieces of grass and a torn leaf. "Maggie, I think you're shaking your fist at a god who doesn't exist."

Maggie stared at him. "But I thought you. . . ."

Mr. Engles held up his hand. "God exists," he said, "but not the god you are afraid to worship." He squinted his eyes at her. "Do you recognize truth, Maggie?" He pressed his hand to his heart. "Do you know what it is to hear something and to know that it is true—that no matter what else, that one thing is true?"

Maggie stared at him. Did she? She searched her mind for something that rang of truth. Some single thing that would not be denied—something that was just . . . there.

"I love you more than anything. . . ."

She stared at Mr. Engles.

". . . except my God."

She continued to stare at him. Then slowly, without wanting to, she nodded her head.

"Then that's what you have to follow," he said.

"You have to follow that one thing you know to be true. Follow it wherever it leads. Hound it to death. Make sense of it. Bring everything else to that one truth and measure it against that standard until you have another truth and then another. Jesus said, 'You shall know the truth and the truth shall set you free.' Forget about your bad god, Maggie. Follow your truth. Your truth isn't God, but it can lead you to God . . . the true God."

The next morning Maggie stood before her kitchen sink staring out the window. She could not remember a time when everything had looked so dry. The sparse rainfall of the summer had resulted in a July already tinged by the golden crispness of August. The lawn around the house was smudged with brown spots and even the green areas were threaded with blades of dry grass. The dry spell had not been able to bleach the green of the grass in the distance, along the bay; but the garden just beyond the lawn looked wilted and sad. The tall grass around the edge was lying flat, and although it was still green, it made crunching sounds when you walked on it. Maggie smelled the acrid sweet aroma of blackberry filling and turned from the window to check the pies.

"Did you hear about Mrs. Engles?" her mother had asked, her voice high and excited as it was whenever she was imparting news of importance, whether good or bad. "She died last night in her sleep, a heart attack, apparently. Mr. Engles didn't even realize it until he woke up this morning. Can you imagine that?"

Maggie set the timer for five more minutes, then turned back to the counter. She stared rigid and dry eyed at the rest of the blackberries still in the sink. She wanted to scream and hurl them at the walls of her tidy, scrubbed kitchen. She wanted to see the ugly black juice running down the wall into a puddle on the floor.

The pies were bubbling over again.

Mr. Engles's eyes seemed large and his face pinched as he stood alone in the doorway of his home when Maggie arrived on his front porch. Maggie reached toward him and he took her into his arms. Maggie let him cry without realizing she was crying also. "It's all right, girl. It's all right," Mr. Engles said, patting her head. "Come sit down here on the couch where we can talk."

"I brought you some pies," Maggie said, wiping her cheeks with the back of her hand. She hurried back to the car to get them. When Mr. Engles saw the pies he squinted his eyes. "Are those the blackberries we picked yesterday?"

Maggie nodded.

Mr. Engles took them from her and set them gently on the counter. He fussed with them, looking for pot holders to put under them so as not to ruin the countertop. He debated whether or not to cover them with foil and finally decided against it. When he was satisfied he had taken proper care of the pies, he motioned for Maggie to follow him into the living room.

Maggie sat on the couch and Mr. Engles low-ered himself beside her. But in a moment Maggie rose to her feet, folded her arms across her chest, and began to pace slowly about the room. Her brow was furrowed and Mr. Engles watched her silently. She knew from experience he would not break in upon her thoughts until she was ready to speak. He never seemed to lose confidence that her thoughts would lead somewhere. And when she was with him, they did. More than at any other time.

The living room was small but comfortable. As Maggie paced back and forth she tried to imagine Mr. Engles living in this house by himself. She remembered Mrs. Engles's constant puttering about, making sure everything was just right for him. There was one time, when Maggie was about eight, that she and Lars had burst into the kitchen, loud and boisterous from their outdoor play. Mrs. Engles had shushed them, her finger pressed tightly against her lip. "Lars," she had said, "you know your father is trying to study. Don't disturb him." She had handed them cookies and sent them outside again.

It has always been like that. Mr. Engles had always seemed a little embarrassed by her fussing. But he would miss it now. The house was still tidy and organized, even after her long illness; but Maggie wondered how long Mr. Engles could keep the intricacies of the Engles household in order. There were doilies on the arms of the couch and plaques on the walls. The doilies would have to be washed and pressed— the plaques dusted. One table was covered with framed photographs. There were pictures of Lars in all stages of development; and there were pictures of what Maggie imagined were aunts, uncles, grandparents, and cousins. She wondered vaguely how long it would take someone to notice if she slipped in a dime-store frame with its picture intact—an unknown model or a movie star.

As Maggie paced back and forth she searched for words of comfort. She had none. For the first time in a long while she wished she were able to use the old words. "God is good. God will comfort you." But she couldn't say things she didn't believe. And she couldn't believe.

Mr. Engles sensed her growing distress. He motioned for her to sit down beside him on the couch. "Yesterday when I got home I fixed Marion a dish of blackberries and cream," he said.

Maggie smiled, grateful for his words—any words.

"I told her I had picked the blackberries with you." Mr. Engles smiled. "Do you know what Marion said? 'That's just like you, Alden. I'm lying here sick unto death and you're out there ready to take up with young Maggie Hanson.'"

Maggie gasped, but Mr. Engles was chuckling softly. "She always teased like that," he said. "She was always telling me how. . . ." He bit his lower lip and waved one hand through the air. "Well, anyway . . . she was pleased with the berries. I told her about your question."

"My question?"

"About whether or not it would be right to worship a bad God. It's an interesting question. Do you know what she said?"

Maggie shook her head.

"She said, 'Well, Alden, I'll just have to ask God

about that.' " Mr. Engles shook his head slowly. "She said it just like that, matter-of-factly, as if she planned to have lunch with him the next day."

Once again Maggie wished she could give the proper response. She knew the right response, she just couldn't give it. She was supposed to shake her head and say, "Isn't that something— she must have known." That was the expected comment. Maggie remained silent.

There was another pause in their conversation as the two of them sat quietly on the couch, each lost in his own thoughts. Then Mr. Engles straightened his back. "I don't think the funeral will be until Saturday. We have to allow time for Lars to get home—"

"Lars?"

Mr. Engles looked into Maggie's face. "Lars will be home for the funeral, Maggie. Even missionaries. . . ."

Maggie rose to her feet. "Of course. I'm sorry. Of course he'll come home." She paced slowly around the room. "It's just that he's been gone so long. It seems strange." She paced restlessly, lost in thought.

Mr. Engles watched Maggie move jerkily around the room. He shook his head and sighed. "If he makes all his connections he'll be here Friday," he said at last.

It was late afternoon when Maggie left Mr. Engles' house. When she got home she was still restless, so she went for a walk in the little woods just south of their house. The ancient forest harbored a number of strange old trees. They were dead—had been dead for hundreds of years. But they still stood there, old and defiant, their very existence defending their right to remain. Their trunks were thick and gray—soft because of their years in the damp, salty forest. Many of the branches were twisted and gnarled, curling downward or inward in a strange, contorted way, as if halfway through life they had become confused as to which way to grow.

On the moss-covered forest floor below the brooding old-timers was a thick outgrowth of young firs and spruce. They looked naive in their coats of bright green, and it seemed to Maggie that they were impatient with the deadly reminders that stood silent and still in their midst.

Maggie knelt to examine the delicate ground cover next to an aging hemlock. The leaves were flat and round, like clover. Dotted here and there were little white blossoms—tiny bell-like flowers so delicate they hung sad and drooping, burdened by the dry heat that had managed to creep into even the forest.

In the middle of the woods was a small backwater surrounded by red alders. By the next month the pond would disappear and the ground would become an unpredictable sponge. But so far the dry spell had not managed to eradicate the still quiet pond, its glassy surface pierced by an occasional dead limb.

The afternoon sunshine slanted through the treetops. In places, the ageless light penetrated to the gray, middle-aged forest floor. Repetition ruled. Seasons and years, decades and centuries had passed as dead branches and decaying tree trunks had bedded down together in gentle layers of rot.

Maggie allowed her body to slump against an ancient tree trunk, her mind a whirl of longing and dread.

His plane was due on Friday.

13 CONFRONTATION

Lars was standing in the vestibule of the tiny church, greeting relatives and old friends. It was almost time for the service to begin, and in the background the organ whined solemn strains of funeral music. He looked terrible. No, he looked glorious. But his skin was the wrong color. The right color, actually—gray.

"What color am I?"

"Gray."

He turned suddenly and Maggie caught her breath. "Maggie," he whispered. His eyes had lost none of their brightness and they pierced into hers with alarming intensity. "How are you?" he asked.

As she looked into his eyes she lifted her chin—almost imperceptibly—but the tightening of muscles around his intense blue eyes told her he had not missed it—her anger. "I'm fine," she said evenly.

"Maggie, I. . . ."

Just then Mr. Engles, wrinkled and pale, approached Lars and touched him on the elbow. "Ah, I see you found her," he said. Mr. Engles took Maggie's hand and she squeezed his gently. "Lars," he said, turning away from her, "Pastor wants us to take our seats. It's almost time for the service to begin. Where's Grandma?" He glanced about, then motioned toward his mother, a little white-haired woman standing off to one side. She tottered toward him, not understanding exactly what it was, but knowing she was wanted.

"It's time for the service, Mother," Mr. Engles said loudly, close to her ear. "Here, take my arm." He reached for her hand and placed it securely on his elbow, covering it with his own. They walked slowly toward the sanctuary. Other family members gathered behind Lars, his father, and his grandmother. They filed into the stuffy sanctuary, taking their places in the front.

Maggie glanced toward the door. It was standing open and the July heat was rising in waves from the sidewalk. The grass along the edges was bleached and dry. It smelled like hay.

Surely Andrew had parked the car by now. She didn't want to walk in late—be conspicuous. Then she heard Andrew's steps in the gravel of the parking lot and a few moments later saw him coming up the walk. He stepped into the vestibule, brushing the hair back from his damp forehead. "Another scorcher," he stated.

"It's time for the service to start," Maggie said. She moved toward the sanctuary.

"Did you see Lars?" Andrew whispered. "How does he look?"

"Fine," Maggie said.

Andrew followed Maggie into the sanctuary and they found two seats toward the back. They slipped into them quietly, but not before Lars had lifted his head and turned around to watch them.

The service was solemn and warm. The words of the pastor and the faces of the mourners were filled with hope—hope stretched to its limits, as only death could stretch it. After the service the mourners gathered in the cemetery, an irregular plot of ground sloping down the hill behind the church.

Lars and his father were standing next to the casket, their heads down, as the pastor intoned the final prayer. The prayer was a long one, and Maggie kept her open eyes fixed on Lars.

What did he think of his God now? Surely even he could see that the God he worshiped was evil—full of wickedness and eager to splash it across the earth and over all the earth's creatures—innocent creatures like his father and mother. But as she studied Lars's face, she was disappointed. His face was solemn, but not angry. Not resentful. Trusting.

After the service, people lingered in the cemetery, visiting and reminiscing. Children wandered among the gravestones, reading the names and dates, exclaiming over those who had died very old, or very young, or very close together. In a far corner several children were playing hide-and-seek, resting their heads against the granite markers as they counted to ten, and then searching for their playmates among the gravestones.

Maggie touched Andrew's sleeve, indicating she was eager to leave. But Andrew said he wanted to talk to Lars. She argued that funerals were a family time—that they shouldn't interfere. She turned to go. But just then Lars broke away from his swarm of relatives and headed toward them. Andrew grabbed Maggie's elbow. "Maggie," he said under his breath, "he's coming. Behave yourself."

"Behave yourself?" She glared at Andrew and then fixed a stony smile on her face as Lars approached.

Lars's smiling eyes shone into hers for a moment; then he turned to Andrew. The old friends embraced each other with rough affection. Then they patted each other on the back and laughed together. Andrew said, "I think I see some gray hair up there," and Lars replied, "You must be pulling yours out, it looks a little sparse." They teased each other and jostled back and forth while Maggie watched in silence. For a moment she was reminded of the bad years—the years Lars, Andrew, and their army of buddies had aligned themselves against her and all that was female. And then she remembered how that had ended—that summer day at the old mausoleum, near the old granite tombstones in the soft summer grass.

"How long will you be home?" Andrew asked now.

"About a week, I think. I want to help Dad get things settled . . . but I can't stay too long. I've had to take extra time off this year anyway and things have piled up. You know how that goes."

Andrew nodded his head, although he had no idea how that went. Andrew never let things pile up. Maggie wondered what sort of things piled up when you were a missionary. For a wild moment she imagined stacks of unsaved souls piling up while Lars took an extra week of vacation.

"Well, listen," Andrew said. "We want you to come out to the house for dinner, don't we, Maggie?" He glanced briefly at Maggie without noticing that she didn't respond. "What night would be best?"

"Well, I . . . I don't know," Lars said. He let his eyes rest uneasily on Maggie. "I don't know. What would be best for you two?" He glanced from one to the other.

"Friday night would be good, wouldn't it, Maggie?" Andrew said eagerly. "Yes, Friday night. Say about five-thirty?"

"Five-thirty?" Maggie said. "You don't get home till six."

"I think I can get off early," Andrew replied. "That's no problem. We haven't seen Lars for years. We want to have all the time we can."

"I can come later," Lars said. "Six—six-thirty?"

"Nope," Andrew said. "I won't hear of it. Five-thirty. Friday night at five-thirty."

The doorbell buzzed and Maggie pressed her trembling fingers against her cheeks. They felt warm. Where was Andrew? He had promised to be home early. *Buzz. Buzz.* Maggie closed her eyes, took a deep breath, and leaned against the counter for a moment. Then she opened her eyes and quickly removed her apron, stopping just a moment to check the pots on the stove.

She was a little breathless when she opened the door.

"Hello, Maggie," Lars said. His sparkling blue eyes warmed her and she involuntarily raised her fingers to her burning cheeks.

"You're early," she blurted. "I mean . . . Andrew's late. Andrew isn't home yet." Lars glanced at his watch. Maggie laughed uneasily. "I'm sorry, come in." She motioned for him to enter.

Lars stepped into the entry, closing the door quietly behind himself. He stood in the tiny hallway and thoughtfully considered his surroundings. He let his eyes wander over the little antique table with its vase of fresh flowers and over the watercolor of Friday Harbor hanging just above it. The gentle gray pastels of the painting—the wharf on a foggy morning—contrasted pleasantly with the vase of delicate yellow roses.

He stared at them a moment, lost in thought. Then he turned his attention to Maggie. "So this is where you live," he said. He leaned back a little and studied Maggie in her setting. "I've tried to imagine it," he commented. "You—the house you live in. . . ." He glanced about again. "It's just right. It suits you."

Maggie shrugged her shoulders. "I suppose so. The house belonged to Andrew's parents. They lived in it when they were first married. It's small, but . . . well, since we have no children. . . ." Maggie's words drifted away and Lars nodded his head in silence. "Well," Maggie said, "how about some lemonade or iced tea?"

"Lemonade sounds wonderful. Is it all right if I look around?"

"Sure."

Lars wandered into the living room and Maggie hurried into the kitchen to fix his lemonade. In a few moments she returned to the living room with two icy drinks. She was watching the ice clink in the glasses.

"Your father says you haven't been well," she said. But then she glanced up and realized the room was empty. Lars had gone into the yard. She could see him through the window. He had stepped off the old brick path and was wandering up and down between the rosebushes—the unkempt rosebushes with their floppy stems. He looked up then and saw Maggie watching him through the window. His gray face brightened. Maggie stepped into the bright July sunshine and handed Lars his lemonade. "Your father says you haven't been well," she repeated. "What did he say—malaria?"

Lars shrugged his shoulders. "Dad worries a lot."

"Under the circumstances, you can hardly blame him," Maggie said. "He had both you and your mother on his mind. Now you're all he has."

Lars nodded. "He'll be all right, don't you think?"

Maggie sat down in one of the lawn chairs and sipped her lemonade thoughtfully. "I think so. He was pretty dependent upon your mother. But he'll be all right."

Lars sat down in the chair opposite Maggie and studied her thoughtfully, taking in the curve of her chin and the way she crossed her legs, her knees squeezed tightly together. "He sure likes you, Maggie. He talks about you all the time." Lars stared at her a moment, his eyes shining and sad. "It runs in the family, I guess."

Maggie rose abruptly. "I think I'd better go check the casserole," she said.

Lars followed her into the kitchen. "Maggie, listen. I need to talk about us—about the past. I know I handled things very badly. I thought we'd have time—but you married Andrew. You got married so soon after . . . for a while I was even afraid you might be pregnant."

Maggie gasped. She slammed a pot holder down on the counter. "You thought I was . . . !" She couldn't even say the word. She pressed her hand against her breast and felt all the anger of the years welling up inside of her. Lars and his God, and his good intentions—and her impulsiveness—swirled around in her brain until she wanted to scream and claw at the impossibleness of his shining blue eyes. There was nothing to talk about. It was all buried in the past and could not be resurrected. Why was he here? Why was he even here?

"Maggie, I don't think you ever understood—"

She whirled on him. "I understood, Lars!"

"You are exposing yourselves to a double standard the boys themselves deny exists."

"I think I understood better than you did," she said quietly. She shook her head. "But it doesn't matter. What does it matter now? Let's just forget it."

Maggie heard the tires of Andrew's car crunching in the gravel.

"I can't, Maggie. Maggie, I. . . ."

Maggie opened the oven door and peered inside. The heat from the oven and the burning of her eyes caused her to blink rapidly, fighting back scalding, angry tears. Lars placed his hands on her shoulders and turned her to face him. She looked into his face and felt his fingers, like hot coals on her shoulders. Her body, her entire body, felt like liquid—fluid and undulating—as though she had no bones. Her bones had disintegrated, along with her anger, and she was lost in the blueness of his shining eyes, shaking her head slowly from side to side, then feeling the increasing pressure of his fingers on her shoulders.

"Maggie, listen," he was saying. "I was hoping. . . . I'm . . . I'm thinking about getting married. I was hoping we could—"

The color drained from Maggie's cheeks and she stepped away from Lars, pressing her back against the counter. Her eyes became hot and dry in their sockets. She stared at him speechlessly—fear, rage, and jealousy bleaching her lips.

She heard Andrew's steps on the sidewalk.

She stared coldly into Lars's eyes. Her lips barely moved as she spoke. "Did it take you all these years to find yourself a virgin?" she said quietly.

The gray of Lars's face turned ashen. "Maggie!" he whispered. "You don't think. . . ."

They stared at each other in the tidiness of Maggie's kitchen, transfixed in the quiet hatred of their love. Andrew burst into the kitchen. "Sorry I'm late," he said.

Maggie turned to the oven and poked a knife in the center of the casserole. Lars glanced at Maggie and then stepped across the room toward Andrew, extending his hand. "That's all right," he said. He took Andrew by the elbow and led him into the living room. "It gave me a chance to make myself at home. You have a nice place—nice wife."

14 "THE GRASS WITHERETH"

Maggie couldn't sleep that night. Rather than try, she decided to take a walk on the beach. Andrew was a sound sleeper and didn't waken when she slipped quietly out of bed. Her beach clothes were hanging in the mudroom off the back porch. She got dressed in the dark and then stepped into the salty night air. The sky was dark, but she could hear the murmur of the waves in the distance and the ground felt secure beneath the soles of her old loafers.

She could only guess when she was at the edge of the garden. Then she felt the tall grass on the other side, and before too long the crunching of gravel beneath her shoes. She had reached the shoreline. She probed her way through the driftwood until her hand touched the surface of a smooth, round log. She scooted herself up onto it and pulled her knees beneath her chin. She sat there, arms wrapped around her legs, with her eyes closed for several moments. Then she opened her eyes, pulled her knees closer to her chest, and looked across the bay to the lights on the opposite shore.

If she could peep into those lighted windows, what would she see? Children gathered on the floor around a late-night game of Scrabble? A husband yelling at his wife because he had no clean socks? A husband and wife snuggled next to the fireplace, chatting quietly?

Nobody built fires in July.

She shifted her gaze from the shoreline to the openness of the sea at the mouth of the bay. She couldn't see anything out there, but she could hear the grinding of the water—the constant ebb and flow, quieter than a roar, but loud in a vast murmuring way. She stared into the darkness and then returned her gaze to the spatter of lights across the bay.

"I'm thinking about getting married. I was hoping. . . ."

Her eyes felt hot and she stared harder. She focused on one tiny flickering light until her eyes burned and strained and felt dry in their sockets. She closed her eyes and let her head drop onto her arm.

"The grass withereth, the flower fadeth. . . ."

Suddenly she lifted her head and stared at the sea—the blackness of the open sea and the dark sky. She squinted her eyes, as if by doing so she could will the darkness to reveal something. Then she tilted her head to one side, like an old man favoring his good ear.

". . . *but the word of the Lord abideth forever.*"

If this is a joke, God, I don't think it's very funny, she thought wildly. Then she remembered she didn't believe in God and couldn't for the life of her imagine what the joke might be. But she continued to stare into the darkness and couldn't rid herself of the notion that out there, somewhere, there was something.

If it wasn't Dr. Trimble's silly double-standard God, or Lars's jealous God, then perhaps it was something else. Some other kind of god. Or nothing. Perhaps it really was just the sea and the sky and the planets and the constellations and the galaxies and the universe.

No jokes.

At least there were no jokes.

Lars returned to South America and the parched summer was followed by one of the soggiest autumns in history. But in early December the weather changed again. The days became sunny and bright, but in the mornings the grass was white with frost. Sometimes it didn't disappear until noon.

It was time for Maggie and Andrew's annual trip to Seattle. Each year in early December they spent a day in Seattle shopping for clothes and Christmas gifts. It was the highlight of the year for Andrew. He checked and rechecked his shopping list and planned their trip down to the tiniest detail, fussing because he couldn't decide where they should eat lunch. Maggie listened to Andrew's plans, frowning and smiling at the appropriate times; but for her it was a way to get their shopping out of the way, nothing more.

The Seattle stores were already busy and bright with the excitement of Christmas. There were children everywhere, laughing and pointing and staring. Something about the Christmas season brought them out from wherever they stayed the rest of the year. They had descended like locusts upon Winter Fantasyland, or whatever the toy department at the Bon Marche was called. They were lined up, on tiptoe, in wriggling, impatient rows, waiting to talk to Santa Claus.

Andrew watched a little girl with blonde curly hair jump from Santa's lap and run back to her mother, whispering that Santa smelled funny— like beer or something. Andrew, amused, covered his mouth with his hand, then repeated the story to Maggie, who, though right next to him, wasn't paying attention to the children. Maggie nodded her head absently, her lips pressed tightly together.

"Where to next?" Andrew asked. Although he was the one with the elaborate shopping list, he was content to follow Maggie from store to store, involving himself somewhat in selecting gifts, but at the same time deferring to Maggie's judgment.

"Well, we've taken care of my mother, your parents, and all the grandparents. That leaves Rachel and her family."

Andrew glanced eagerly toward Winter Fantasyland. "Let's go look at toys for Peter and Annie," he said.

Maggie sighed. "Oh, all right."

They entered Winter Fantasyland through the

white gate. As they walked down the aisle, Andrew impulsively pulled a Raggedy Ann doll from the shelf and handed it to Maggie. "Here, Margaret," he said, arranging the doll in her arms as if it were a real baby, "see how this feels." He stepped back and eyed her approvingly. "It looks good," he said. "You'd still make a good mother."

Maggie frowned and thrust the doll back at Andrew. "Don't be silly," she said, glancing around to see if people were watching. She started down the aisle again.

Why can't he get it through his head that we aren't going to have any children—ever?

Andrew followed her down the aisle and tentatively raised the forbidden subject. "Maybe I should go see another doctor," he said.

Maggie tried to control her irritation. "You know that won't make any difference."

"Well, then you . . . maybe you should. . . ." He let his voice trail off when he realized Maggie had walked over into the next aisle and was reading the instructions on a Punch-and-Stick book.

Maggie couldn't stand it one more minute. She wanted to shut him up—once and for all. When was he going to give up?

What if he didn't? What if he just kept after her with his little questions and suggestions until she was white haired and in her rocking chair? She couldn't stand it. She just couldn't stand it any longer.

Maggie looked at Andrew, at his confused, eager face. He wasn't going to leave her alone. *"See another doctor, Maggie. Just try one more.*

One more. One more." She was going to have to tell him. There was no other way to shut him up for good.

But how could she? She felt trapped and reckless, like she knew she was going to do something terrible but was helpless to stop herself—didn't want to stop herself. She put the Punch-and-Stick book back on the rack and turned to face Andrew. "Andrew, I think there's something you ought to know."

Andrew's face was expectant, his eyes innocent and trusting. "What?" he asked.

Maggie glanced around Winter Fantasyland. *Here? Here in the midst of noisy, excited children—with Christmas carols floating through the air and the occasional ho-ho-ho of a half-drunk Santa Claus? Can I tell him here?*

Could she tell him anywhere?

She looked at Andrew's eager, hope-filled face. *He probably half expects me to tell him I'm pregnant,* she thought. She was filled with disgust and guilt. There was a ringing in her ears and a grayness all around.

"Andrew," she said, "there aren't going to be any children—ever."

"Why? What do you mean? The doctors haven't said. . . ."

She shook her head. "No." She waved her hand back and forth in front of his face. "Remember when I came to the specialist here in Seattle— when I stayed overnight at the hospital?"

Andrew nodded his head. "Did the doctors find something you never told. . . ."

If it hadn't been for the buzzing in her ears she

might have taken her cue from Andrew—made up a story about what the doctors had said. Instead she shook her head and stepped closer to Andrew. She spoke softly, so the couple farther down the aisle wouldn't be able to overhear. "I don't want children, Andrew. I never wanted children. I . . . I had an operation." She shook her head slowly from side to side, as she had in her dream long ago. "We can't have any—ever," she said.

Andrew stared at her, unable at first to comprehend what she'd said. Then the color drained from his lips. A coldness she'd never seen before filled his eyes and chilled her being. Without meaning to, Maggie backed away from him. She watched as he spun around and stalked down the aisle, away from her, his arms swinging wide and stiff at his sides. He inadvertently knocked some Matchbox cars from the shelf. They went clattering across the floor. Instead of stopping to pick them up, Andrew gave his arm an additional thrust which sent some adjacent Tonka trucks crashing across the aisle. Maggie stared after him in horror.

Andrew went down the escalator to the ground floor and then out of the store into the bustling clamor of downtown Seattle. Maggie followed him. He headed toward the wharf. She tried to walk beside him, but he didn't adjust his stride to hers. Every few steps she had to make a quick little dash to keep up with him.

When they reached the ferry depot, Andrew marched up to the ticket counter. "One ticket to San Juan Island," he said to the clerk.

Maggie stared at him in confusion. *One?* Andrew walked away without looking at her. She reached into her purse and counted her money. She had just enough.

"One ticket to San Juan," she said.

They waited for the ferry in silence, not exactly together. Maggie kept him in sight, but Andrew refused to acknowledge her presence. It was the same when they boarded the boat.

As the ferry slid through the waters of Elliott Bay and then out into the Strait of San Juan de Fuca, Andrew moved restlessly from place to place—first staring over the rail at Seattle's receding skyline, and then sitting inside, looking uncomfortably confined, in one of the lounge chairs. In a few moments he climbed the noisy metal stairs to the cafeteria for a cup of coffee. Maggie followed him to the cafeteria but she didn't have enough money left to buy anything.

She watched him carry his cup of coffee to one of the far tables. He sat staring vacantly at the passing scenery. Maggie wandered back to the outer deck, pulled her coat collar close to her neck, and leaned her elbows on the icy metal rail. The sun was yellow-white in the blue December sky. The chill wind burned her cheeks and snatched her breath away. The sun shone on the water in blinding radiance, like millions of twinkling lights. Farther out the current forced the lights into clusters and moved them in irregular rows of brightness. Maggie stared at the center of brightness until her eyes hurt, trying to see the movement of the water behind the glare. She could see the water moving toward the blazing reflection on one side, and away from it on the other. But in the center, at the point where the sun shined directly onto the water, she could see only brightness—overwhelming, beautiful, eye-scorching brightness. She wished she could disappear into it, vanish, no longer exist.

They were passing a tiny island and Maggie lifted her eyes to the shoreline. The skeleton trees along the water were silhouetted in layers against the dark and hazy hillside in the distance.

Maggie squinted at the scene before her and felt she had to order it somehow—get it under control—break it into pieces small enough for her to handle. Like a painter. What colors would she use? Blue for the water, just a shade darker than the wide expanse of sky, and blue-black for the trees along the shore. Or brown? More brown than black. And the brightness would be . . . white? Not white exactly. She stared into the glare of sunlight. Not white, exactly, but not yellow, certainly. White with the tiniest hint of blue. But in the center, at the very core of brightness, she couldn't see even a tinge of blue. She stared and stared at it, trying to see if it actually was white. Her eyes began to water, but still she stared at it. It wasn't white. Her eyes burned and she closed them, squeezing her eyelids together until tears spilled over.

I'll probably go blind.

Maggie shook her head. Why couldn't she have loved him? She saw his pale, drawn face, his eyes hollowed out by her deceit, and in that moment— her eyes burning in their sockets and Andrew's ashen image etched in her mind—she loved him with a love as fierce as the sunlight on the water was bright. Andrew. Whatever would she do without Andrew?

Why couldn't she have given him children, the only thing he had ever—in all ten years of their marriage—really asked for? She stared at the yellow, white water. She didn't know. It had just seemed impossible.

Impossible? More impossible than living the rest of her life without him?

15 "BROKEN, LIKE VOWS"

It was less than a mile from the ferry depot to their little house along the shore. They walked along the road with only the crunching of their shoes on the gravel breaking the silence. It was cold. Their breath formed miniature clouds. Andrew kept a pace or two ahead of Maggie, and Maggie made no attempt to catch up.

When they got to the house they could hear the telephone ringing inside. Andrew jammed his key into the lock and ground it to the left. He shoved the door open and stepped inside, ignoring the telephone. Maggie rushed past him and lifted the receiver. It was her mother and she was using her high, squeaky voice. "Have you heard?" she asked.

Maggie was watching Andrew open the living room drapes. He yanked the cord so hard she feared it would break. "No," she said. "What?"

"They announced it at our missionary circle

this morning. I just couldn't believe it."

Maggie sighed and rolled her eyes to the ceiling. "What, Mother?"

Her mother hesitated. "Are you all right, Maggie? You sound funny. Is Andrew there?"

"Yes, Andrew's here."

"Maybe . . . let me talk to Andrew."

Maggie held the receiver away from her ear and stared at it, then mumbled, "OK," into the mouthpiece.

"Andrew," Maggie called, "Mother wants to talk to you."

Andrew's eyes met hers for just a moment and Maggie turned away. *If he believed in murder he'd kill me,* she thought. Then she wondered how many murderers actually believed in murder. It wasn't like believing in God. You didn't become converted to murder. She imagined a testimony meeting at Leavenworth—a bulky pock-faced man in light blue denims rising to his feet shyly. "Well, I was converted to murder when I was thirteen. . . ."

"I don't believe it," Andrew was saying. "We knew he had been sick, but. . . . " He pulled a chair away from the table and slumped in it. "Um . . . um." Andrew's face was white and contorted—not angry, as it had been in the toy department, but filled with the same disbelief. Maggie was afraid he was going to cry. "OK. OK. I'll tell her, Mom. No, she'll be all right. . . . OK. Thanks for calling."

Andrew hung up the phone and sat staring at the floor, his arms hanging between his legs. He lifted his eyes to the ceiling and moved his hands up and down in a movement without rhythm or meaning. Finally he looked at Maggie. The bitterness in his face was mixed with pity. "Lars is dead," he said. "He died early this morning." He shook his head.

Maggie stared at Andrew as he spoke. She couldn't hear his words. She could see his lips moving but she couldn't hear any sound, just a mild buzzing, like a telephone left off the hook. A buzzing in her ears and something about the room. Like a silent movie—black and white.

Something rising in her throat. She gagged, turned, and vomited into the sink.

Andrew had held her forehead once. He had stood next to her as she was hanging over the toilet and had placed one hand on her shoulder, the other on her forehead, as her mother had done when she was a child. But now Andrew rose to his feet and stalked from the kitchen. He slammed the front door so hard the vase toppled from the little antique table in the entryway and crashed to the floor, breaking into sharp, tiny pieces of colored glass.

Maggie wiped her lips on a paper towel before walking into the hallway. She knelt beside the shattered pieces of glass, then started to pick them up. There were too many. She couldn't remember how to clean up broken glass. There was a way. Her mother had shown her. *"Stand back, Maggie, you might cut yourself. Don't touch the glass."* Maggie picked up several pieces of the shattered glass and stared at them.

Broken like vows.

"I will mother your children, and stay with

you always, a faithful helpmeet, friend, and lover."

She slowly squeezed her fingers into the glass. Tighter and tighter. She could see the blood. Finally she could feel the pain. *"I will mother your children."* She clenched her hands together, the bloody one inside the other, and hunched forward, sobbing.

At least she hadn't mothered someone else's.

It took the doctor over an hour to pick the shreds of glass from her skin. "How did you do this?" he asked as he peered at her hand beneath the glaring light.

"Just cleaning up some broken glass," Maggie said. "I was careless, I guess."

The doctor glanced at her face. "You should be more careful," he said. "Some of these are pretty deep."

"Um," Maggie said.

Andrew was waiting for her next to the receptionist's desk. The waiting room was only partially lit, not bright and shadowless as during regular hours. Andrew rose to his feet when Maggie and the doctor stepped out of the examination room. "She'll be all right," the doctor said to him. "I didn't take any stitches. I think I got all the glass." He patted Maggie on the shoulder. "You need to be more careful, young lady." Maggie pulled her shoulder away from his hand. He didn't seem to notice. "Call me if you have any trouble," he said.

Maggie and Andrew walked to the car in silence. One more strike against her—having to call the doctor after hours. She supposed he was keeping score.

Maggie wasn't sure who had notified Rachel. But Rachel phoned the next morning wondering when the funeral would be. "It will be on the island, won't it?"

"Yes," Maggie said. "It's Friday. Would you like to stay with us? You are coming, aren't you?"

"Yes. But I'll have to bring the kids. Are you sure you won't mind?"

"No, of course not."

The more people the better, she thought. The silence between her and Andrew wouldn't be so loud.

Rachel took the spare bedroom. The kids planned to sleep in sleeping bags on the living room floor.

"We go camping," little Annie announced at the dinner table.

"Camping!" Andrew exclaimed. "Aren't you afraid of bears?"

Peter glanced at Andrew, then leaned toward Annie protectively, looking into her pixie-sweet face. "It's not camping, really, Annie—it's *like* camping. We get to sleep in our sleeping bags, that's all."

"I told them it would be kind of like camping," Rachel explained.

"Bears?" Annie said, ignoring Peter and her mother and staring at Andrew, her eyes big and round.

"I was just teasing, Annie," Andrew said, motioning for her to come sit on his lap. Andrew pulled her plate next to his and she finished her dinner there, perched on his knee, chatting about bears and alligators and other wild things.

Andrew didn't speak to Maggie all during dinner. He said only a few words to Rachel. After dinner he took the children into the living room and gave them horseback rides. He crawled around the floor on all fours, bucking them off his back and laughing with them as they tumbled onto the carpet.

Rachel watched Andrew and the children from the doorway for several minutes. Then she returned to the kitchen where Maggie was trying to wash dishes with one hand. Rachel's eyes were sparking with anger.

"Maggie—," she began.

"Save it," Maggie said.

The doorbell rang. Maggie waited for Andrew to answer it. When he continued roughhousing with the children, Maggie excused herself and went into the hallway. When she opened the door, her mother bustled into the house, complaining of the cold and apologizing for not calling ahead. "I took a casserole over to Mr. Engles," she said. "I thought maybe you could use these." She handed Maggie a plastic bag of chocolate chip cookies. Tragedies brought out the best in Mrs. Hanson—filled her body with energy and her mind with countless good deeds. "Little ones have to have their cookies, don't they?" she said, stooping over and talking toward the children in baby talk. Then she straightened her back and turned to Maggie. "Have you seen her?" she asked. She was using her high, squeaky voice.

"Samantha, I mean. I think she looks a little like you."

"Mother. . . ."

"Really. Someone else mentioned it. One of the ladies from church. She said, 'You know, Lars's fiancée reminds me of your Maggie.' Isn't that funny?"

"I have a very common face, Mother. People are always telling me I look like someone they know."

"Well, I suppose. But, anyway, it's certainly too bad. She seems like a very nice lady. Her first husband was a missionary pilot—killed in a plane crash. This must be very hard on her. And then Lars, you know. All those years alone. Finally when he finds someone—it's sad. Very sad."

"Yes," Maggie said. It probably was. But it was hard for her to feel any sympathy for the woman she'd run into so unexpectedly at the church.

Lars's chalk-white face.

"Did it take you all these years to find yourself a virgin?"

Even then he hadn't found one. Her husband had been killed in a plane crash. Well, that was respectable, at least. The wife of a missionary pilot. Not like someone who would romp in the basement of a music building.

"What happened to your hand, Maggie?" her mother asked.

"Oh, nothing." Maggie waved her bandaged hand through the air nonchalantly. "I just cut myself cleaning up a broken vase."

Mrs. Hanson pulled her eyebrows together and glanced at Rachel. "I always told her to be careful with broken glass," she said. Maggie could see she wanted to give her broken glass speech, but instead she rattled on about the funeral. Lars's death and the arrival of his fiancée was big news on the island. The romance of it, combined with the recent death of Lars's mother, seemed the greatest of tragedies. The telephone lines crisscrossing the island buzzed with the news.

"Well, at least he didn't have any children," her mother was saying. "It would be even more tragic if he had left a little family behind."

"Yes, I suppose so," Maggie said. She was careful not to meet Rachel's eyes.

"Death is so hard to explain to children," Mrs. Hanson continued wistfully.

As if she'd ever tried. When had she even tried?

"I think I'd better get those kids ready for bed," Rachel said, excusing herself.

"I need to be going too," Mrs. Hanson said, moving toward the door. "Would you like me to pick you and Rachel up for the funeral? Is Andrew going straight from work?"

Maggie opened the door and walked her to her car. "No, I think he'll come home to clean up first. He's one of the pallbearers. He needs to be there a little early. Come to think of it, maybe you could pick up Rachel and the children. I have to be there early too. Mr. Engles asked if I would sit with him. I can ride with Andrew."

"Mr. Engles asked you to sit with him? Isn't that a little odd? Well, he always did seem to like you. What about Samantha? Is she sitting with the family? These things can be so awkward."

Maggie wasn't sure what her mother found

awkward. Funerals? Families? Fiancées?

"I don't know," Maggie said. "He didn't mention Samantha." Maggie sensed a tiny victory. She lavished it upon herself.

"Well, it's cold out here," her mother said. "You'd better get inside. I'll see you tomorrow."

16 PROMISES

When Maggie awoke the next morning, Andrew's side of the bed was disheveled and empty. He had already left for work. Rachel and the children were still asleep, so she pulled the covers tighter around her and stared at the drizzle lingering outside her bedroom window. She lay very still beneath the covers, watching the drops lined up heavily along the edge of the eaves. Everything was gray—the grayness of Lars, draping itself over the day and dripping from the sky. She tried to guess which drop would be the next to fall from the eaves. They became elongated, bottom heavy just before they fell, but she could never guess the right one.

After a few minutes she glanced at the clock. It was early. She had time for a walk on the beach before the funeral. She didn't bother to eat breakfast. Instead she donned her baggy beach clothes and her bright yellow rain slicker.

She was the only bright spot on the gray, drizzly shore. Sea gulls were standing like statues on the sand, their spindle-straight legs supporting their plump bodies in comical majesty. There were occasional gulls gliding above the surface of the water, dipping and swooping as if performing to music. Maggie watched a lone gull rise until it was high in the gray sky. It soared there, on the breathy, still note of a flute. The tempo changed and, against a rising crescendo, the gull turned downward, slicing through the horizon in a purposeful dive. It swooped into the water and came up with a silvery fish.

He had been searching for his breakfast.

There was no music.

Maggie climbed down the short embankment and stumbled through the litter of drift logs high on the beach. The tide was out, and after trudging past the logs and through the dry sand high on the beach, she came to the tide pools and half-submerged rocks at the edge of the surf. As she walked in the soggy sand, the muck sucked at her boots. She left a soft snail trail of footprints behind herself.

She stooped to finger the barnacles on the same rock she and Mr. Engles had studied so long ago. Were they the same barnacles? But then as she looked up to watch the incoming waves, she was assailed by another memory.

She saw herself and Lars chasing each other through the shallow breakers. Unlike today, it had been sunny and bright. She and Lars had been sunbathing. In the midst of some silly argument, Maggie had thrown a handful of sand at him.

"OK for you," Lars had said. He picked up a handful of sand and drew back his arm.

Maggie scooted away from him, then dashed down the beach. The sand beneath the soles of her bare feet was warm and soft and she ran in a slogging fashion, the pull of the soft sand working against the energy of her young body. Lars was close behind her as she ran toward the ocean, toward the hard, cold sand along the water's edge. As the sand became more solid beneath her feet, she was able to pick up speed. But so was Lars. Soon Lars had her trapped between the icy waters of the strait and his raised fistful of sand.

"Eeek, eek," Maggie cried with mock helplessness, "the Mugger's going to get me!"

Lars nodded his head savagely and threatened her with his fistful of sand. He bared his teeth and made growling sounds. Maggie walked backward away from him until she could feel the ocean foam soft against her heels. Then a tiny wave crept silently across the sand and covered her feet with biting cold. The pain was excruciating. She turned suddenly and ran into the ocean, jumping over the incoming waves until the water reached her knees. Then she turned to face Lars. "Don't do it," she said. "You might get sand in my eyes. I hate getting sand in my eyes."

"Ooh, poor thing," Lars mocked. "And I suppose you think I like it?"

"I didn't get it in your eyes!"

"Well, you could have."

Maggie backed away from him. "No, Lars, please. Don't." She held up her hand. "I promise. I won't do it again."

"Ever?"

"Ever."

"Say it."

"What?"

"Say, 'I will never throw sand at Lars again for as long as I live.' "

Maggie didn't hesitate. "I will never. . . ."

Lars held up his hand to interrupt her. "Now, Maggie, I want you to understand the seriousness of this. We might live to be very, very old. Suppose when we are ninety-three we come down here for a little walk on the beach and you feel an impulse to throw sand at me. What will you do?"

"Oh," Maggie said, shaking her head solemnly, "I will with unbelievable self-control overcome the urge." She waved one hand through the air. "I will never, ever, for as long as I live, throw sand at you again."

Lars squinted at her warily. "You won't forget?"

Maggie shook her head. "Never. I will never forget."

"Well," Lars said, "well . . . I guess I can trust you." He opened his fist and let the sand sift into the ocean. Then he stooped over to rinse his damp palm of clinging grains. While he was stooped over, Maggie quickly reached into the water and came up with a fistful of dripping sand. She aimed it at Lars's back. When he felt the cold sand splatter against his warm back he jerked upright in disbelief.

"Maggie!" he said. He looked really angry.

Maggie started to back away. She was laughing, her eyes dancing in mischief. "I had my fingers crossed," she said. "See?" She pulled her left hand from behind her back and showed him her crossed fingers.

"That's it!" Lars said. "You have gone too far." He started toward Maggie. But just then a wave hit him, nearly knocking him off balance. He lowered his head and, more determined than ever, lunged toward Maggie. She backed away from him, but the water pulled at her legs and she was only able to move a few inches at a time. Suddenly Lars shouted, "Maggie, look out!"

He was too late. A huge wave had sneaked up behind Maggie. It hit her just below her shoulder blades and swept her off her feet. Lars had just enough time to laugh a startled laugh before he too was bobbing in the briny, icy water, flailing his legs back and forth in a desperate attempt to ground himself. He felt something, opened his eyes, and realized it was Maggie's arm. He grabbed it.

A few moments later the wave rushed back out to sea and left them stranded upon the sand, screaming and laughing. Lars pulled Maggie to her feet and they stared at each other. Their bodies were gritty with salt and their hair was clinging in soppy strands about their heads. Maggie brushed her bangs from her forehead and looked into Lars's laughing eyes. She stood on her tiptoes and kissed him quickly on the lips. "I heard you," she said. "You tried to warn me. You actually tried to warn me. Now I know for sure you love me."

"Don't be fooled," Lars said. "I was just hoping

you'd turn and get the wave full in your face."

Maggie laughed, then shivered. "Let's go get dried off."

As they walked back to the blanket, Lars turned to her, his face a mask of confusion. "You. . . ." He stopped walking. He planted his feet firmly in the sand and stared at Maggie, his hands on his hips. "You threw sand at me," he said. "You promised you would never, ever throw sand at me again for as long as we both shall live, and then you turned right around and threw sand at me! Have you no moral fiber whatsoever?"

Maggie stared back at him, undaunted. "I told you," she said, "I had my fingers crossed. It doesn't count if you have your fingers crossed."

Lars sputtered in exasperation, "Well, how was I to know? I didn't know you had your stupid fingers crossed. Here I was thinking you were making a solemn vow and all the time you had your fingers crossed." He was almost angry. "I can't stand that!"

"That's the beauty of it," Maggie said. "The other person doesn't know." She lifted her hands in the air helplessly. "That's just the way it works. Crossing your fingers is a very one-sided business."

"You can say that again," he replied.

Maggie pressed the side of her hand against the barnacles on the rock until the pain was unbearable.

"Now, Maggie, I want you to understand the seriousness of this. We might live to be very, very old. Suppose when we are ninety-three you are

overcome with a sudden impulse to throw sand at me. What will you do?"

Maggie picked up a nearby stick and began poking at the barnacles. She poked and jabbed at them. Harder and harder. *"What will you do?"* She began hitting the rock with the stick, again and again.

"We might live to be very, very old. What will you do? What will you do?"

I don't know. She pounded the rock with the stick. *I don't know. I don't know what I'll do.*

"People shouldn't make promises they can't keep."

"I will mother your children and will stay with you always, a faithful helpmeet, friend, and lover." She slumped down onto the rock. She let the stick fall to the ground and her shoulders hunched forward in silent sobs. *"Crossing your fingers is a very one-sided business."* She sobbed quietly in the gray morning drizzle until it was time to leave for the funeral.

17 EULOGY

The sanctuary was nearly full. It was surprising how many people had come to pay their respects to Lars—he had been away from the community for over ten years. Maggie supposed most of them had come for Mr. Engles's sake, not in memory of Lars. Mr. Engles had lost his son and his wife within a few months of each other—people were sensitive to that sort of thing.

The air was sweet with flowers and with the hushed unreality of formal grief. As Maggie sat stiffly in the front pew next to Mr. Engles, she congratulated herself. The quiet rigidness of her stomach told her she was doing fine. Just fine. She reached over and patted Mr. Engles's hand.

She had spotted Samantha when they walked in. She was seated on the other end of the pew behind them. It was strange that Mr. Engles had asked her, instead of Samantha, to sit with him. But then, he could never quite forget the old days. Mr. Engles, more than anyone else, remembered the Maggie and Lars of long ago—the Maggie and Lars who had run freely together in their young bodies, innocent and unafraid. He knew them in their childish bodies, young and free, and he knew them in their lover bodies—yearning and joyful. But he had not known them in their fear-filled bodies. He had not seen them in the lobby of the boys' dormitory, their faces grotesque and distorted—gargoyles filled with devils and alienated by fear.

Maggie stared at the awful tan coffin and tried to enter into the meaning of the service. Grief had come so easily that morning on the gray drizzly beach. But here, in the hushed quiet of the sanctuary, in the midst of programmed sorrow, she felt nothing. What was wrong with her? Why did she always do things at the wrong time and in the wrong places?

It was time for the eulogy.

Without introduction, an elderly white-haired man made his way to the platform. As he walked toward the pulpit, Maggie squeezed her finger-nails into the palms of her hands. The old gentle-man centered himself behind the podium, gripping the sides of the pulpit with either hand, and then stared at the congregation, his fiery eyes studying the faces before him. Finally he spoke.

"I first met Lars Engles when he was in college," he said.

Maggie felt hot and sweaty. Her fingers were trembling as she stared at the unopened program in her hand. She opened it slowly. "In memory of Lars G. Engles," it said. Her eyes moved down the page.

"Presentation of the Eulogy: Dr. Ralph Trimble."

Maggie shut the program quickly and squeezed her eyes together. She entwined her shaking fingers, trying to hold them still.

Mr. Engles glanced at her, his face concerned. He reached over and took her left hand in his. Maggie squeezed his hand tightly and didn't let go.

". . . He was a young man with all the fire and passion typical of the young. But he was a young man with a difference. Overriding all the dreams, desires, goals, and ambitions of this young man was a passion and love for his God. Physically he died a young man. But this death, this physical death which we have come here today to acknowledge, is not the real death. The real death took place ten years ago when Lars was still in college. That was when Lars really died—when he died to himself. He surrendered himself to God. He lifted himself up to God and invited God to put to death anything in his life that would separate him from the God he worshiped and adored. . . ."

Maggie stared at Dr. Trimble. Her eyes filled with tears and she stared and stared at him, afraid that if she blinked, the water in her eyes would spill down her cheeks. She squeezed Mr. Engles's hand and tried to control her breathing. What was he saying? What did he mean? Maggie squeezed her eyelids together and pressed her arms close against the sides of her body. Her chest felt constricted—passion, regret, pride, and hatred were wedged together in confusion.

". . . That death was not an easy death—it was not a quick death—it was a living sacrifice. I can truly say of Lars Engles that he poured out his life, a living sacrifice." Dr. Trimble leaned forward and stared at the audience. His eyes rested briefly on Maggie, moved away, and then moved back to her face again, as if remembering something. His voice increased in intensity. "But in the process Lars came to know his God in a way that few men do. He came to trust his God. Completely."

Dr. Trimble paused a moment. He brushed his hand across his cheeks. "I loved Lars Engles," he said. He cleared his throat. "I want to read something to you this morning. It is a page from Lars's prayer journal." Dr. Trimble droned on. The voice was his, but the words were Lars's: "More than anything I want to participate in your plan for this earth. While I live on this earth, Lord, I want to be in on whatever it is you are about. Help me to understand your love and your power. Help me to understand your ways. Help me to line up my desires with your desires. . . ."

For a fragile moment Maggie imagined that all her years of bitterness had been unnecessary. There was something . . . something about her desires, and God's desires. Could they be the same—really?

Dr. Trimble read on. But for Maggie it was too much, all of it—this funeral, all the years, Dr. Trimble showing up with Lars and the awful tan coffin. She wanted to throw herself across the top of the casket. In a final frenzied act of passion—like in a B-grade movie—she wanted to pound her fists on the top of the coffin and scream a protest against all the things she didn't understand. Demand a hearing. *Explain to me! I want to understand!*

"Do you know what truth is, Maggie? Follow after it. Hound it to death. Make sense of it."

Tell me. Tell me.

But it was too late. Lars had been her truth. Lars had been her tiny fragment of truth. And he was gone.

Maggie thought of Lars's body lying stiff and cold inside the coffin. A body with no one inside. Where was he? Could he see her? Could he see inside her right now and know that all her anger and bitterness really didn't count at all? That she still loved him with all her being—that she would never, ever understand any of it. That she would never understand why he couldn't love her and God at the same time. That she would never understand how he could love a God she despised—hated—hated because he would not let her have what she wanted.

She had a brief image of herself screaming at her mother—screaming and stomping her feet. Her mother was holding a pop bottle out of her reach.

"No, Margaret, no. It would hurt you."

Still Maggie screamed and pleaded. Finally her mother calmed her down enough to make her listen.

"Come here, Margaret. Smell this. See? It's not really pop. It's kerosene. I was using it to wash the windows."

Maggie had pressed her nose to the bottle and pulled away in disgust.

The pastor closed the service. Andrew and the other pallbearers carried the coffin from the sanctuary. They slipped around in the mud as they carried it to the burial plot. They buried Lars beside his mother on the slope behind the church. There were no children playing tag among the tombstones. It was raining too hard.

18 HOUNDING TRUTH

After the service Andrew returned to work and Maggie went to the bank. Rachel and the children spent the afternoon at Andrew's parents. When Maggie got home from work she had a little time before she needed to start dinner.

She headed for the beach.

When she reached the shore she returned to the old barnacle-covered rock. She sat on a nearby log and picked up a piece of driftwood. She tapped it lightly against the tiny fortresses.

"I love you more than anything . . . except my God . . . except my God . . . except my God."

The dark hills on the opposite shore were silhouetted against the late afternoon sky. The sun had finally broken through and was proclaiming a final protest against the heavy clouds. It shot long golden stripes across the sky and over the surface of the water before disappearing behind the darkened slopes. Maggie watched the layered clouds turn flame red and then dim to gentle amber as the sun surrendered to the horizon. Darkness crept across the sky and finally smothered the last flicker of daylight. The deepening sky blended into the dark hills and then merged with the briny blue-black water of the bay.

As Maggie watched the night drain the scene of color, she could hear the gentle waves lap against the nearby shore. The rhythm was as soothing as the sky was deep. She leaned her head against the driftwood log and closed her eyes.

You're there, aren't you?

In an ancient rhythm the waves continued to slap gently against the pebbles along the beach.

*This far you may come and no farther—
this is where your proud waves halt.*

I don't understand. Do you understand that I don't understand?

"Follow it wherever it leads. Hound it to death. Make sense of it."

Maggie shook her head.

When Maggie returned to the house she was surprised to find it dark. But Andrew's pickup was in the driveway. She walked into the living room and switched on the light. Andrew was sitting on the couch, his head back, his eyes closed.

"Hi," Maggie said. "Sorry I'm late. I took a walk on the beach."

Andrew didn't reply. She wasn't surprised.

She fixed them a light supper. They ate it in silence. Finally Andrew spoke. "Rachel and the kids staying here tonight?"

Maggie nodded. "Your folks are bringing them by after dinner."

"Good."

When Rachel and the children arrived, Andrew invited his parents in. The family gathered noisily in the living room.

"How about making some popcorn, Maggie?" Andrew called. He was already down on all fours wrestling with Peter and Annie.

Maggie nodded and went into the kitchen. She was glad to be alone. Alone in the kitchen. She really wanted to be all alone—like Lars. Alone in his coffin. She wondered what it would be like in there with him. Would his presence fill the coffin as it had filled her tiny scrubbed kitchen last summer? No. His presence was no longer there. Still, it seemed strange to think of his body buried, cold and alone beneath the soil. Did Mr. Engles think about things like that? What it was like for his son and his wife to lie beneath the cold, soggy soil? Probably not. He imagined angels.

When Maggie returned to the living room, she was surprised to see Andrew had talked the whole family into a game of King Elephant. They were all seated in a circle on the floor—even his mother, her legs folded under her awkwardly. Probably never get up again.

"Come on, Maggie," Rachel said. "There's room for you right here by Annie."

Maggie waved her hand in refusal. "No, I don't

think so," she said. She wrinkled her forehead, as if she'd suddenly remembered something important. "Andrew, do you . . . do you think someone should go check on Mr. Engles? Is he by himself?"

"Huh? I don't know." He didn't look at her as he spoke.

"Surely someone is with him," Andrew's mother said. "I don't think you need to worry about him. Why don't you come play King Elephant with us?"

Maggie scratched her head. "I don't know," she said. "I think maybe I'd better run over there."

"Really?" Andrew said, glancing up briefly. A bitter smile edged his lips. "Well, whatever you think is best."

It was just a little less than a mile to Mr. Engles's house. The headlights of her car pierced the dark, cold night. Maggie shivered as she pulled into his driveway.

There was one small light burning inside his house. No cars. He was alone. She imagined him hunched on the couch, wondering if it was late enough to go to bed.

She knocked on the door. It was a few moments before he answered. When he opened the door, Mr. Engles blinked his red, watery eyes and then reached his frail arms toward her. He held her in his arms for several moments and then straightened his small, brittle back.

"Oh, Maggie," he said, wiping his hand across his cheeks. "I'm so glad you came by. I did a very foolish thing." He led her into the living room. "Pastor suggested I have someone stay with me tonight, but I told him I'd be OK."

He led Maggie to the couch and they sat down. "But then . . . then I started going through some of Lars's things. . . ." He shook his head and wiped his nose with the back of his hand. Maggie searched in her purse for a handkerchief. Finally she noticed a box of tissues on the table. She brought it to him and set it on his bony knees. "Thank you," he said. He blew his nose, then shook his head from side to side. "I should never have done that."

Maggie nodded her head. She thought of herself, wallowing through her box of souvenirs— the token from the penny arcade and the fragile ring of dried grass. She bit her lip and took one of Mr. Engles's hands in her own. She patted it softly. "There'll be time for that," she said. "Don't rush things."

Mr. Engles nodded.

They sat together in silence for a few moments and then Maggie rose to her feet. She began pacing around the room. Tears were welling up inside of her. She bit her lip, trying to hold them back. Mr. Engles came beside her and handed her a tissue. He put his arm around her waist and together they paced back and forth across the thin braided carpet. Sorrow flowed between them, neither of them knowing who suffered more.

When Mr. Engles could feel that some of the tension had drained from Maggie's body, he led her to the couch and they sat down again. He looked into her face for a long, quiet time as the pieces of the ancient puzzle slipped partially into place. Finally he said, "You still love him, don't you?" She lifted her tear-filled eyes to his and nodded. Tears coursed down her cheeks and she threw herself into his arms. As she wept he brushed his fingers through her hair. "He loved you too, Maggie," he whispered. "He always loved you."

Maggie shook her head.

"He never. . . ." Mr. Engles cleared his throat. "He never talked to me about it—Lars was never one to confide—but he always asked about you in his letters. And when you got married he . . . he disappeared. The college called to see if he'd come home. He was gone for nearly a month. Nobody heard a word from him. I never did know where he'd been . . . not until today."

"Today?"

"Dr. Trimble told me. He'd hitchhiked all the way to Chicago—to see Dr. Trimble. Dr. Trimble has had quite an influence on him, I guess."

Maggie's face was pale, her voice even. "Yes, I know," she said.

Mr. Engles shrugged his bony shoulders. "They kept in touch—all through the years. Dr. Trimble had a great deal of respect for Lars." Mr. Engles ran his fingers through his wispy white hair. "You know, I guess a father always hopes his son will confide in him. We want to see ourselves as sage advisors, I suppose, but children have a way of seeking someone else when they want advice. It hurts in a way . . . but I doubt that Lars could have had a wiser mentor than Dr. Trimble. Although . . ." Mr. Engles wagged his finger through the air, "although Trimble seemed to feel he'd failed Lars somehow." Mr. Engles shook his head in puzzlement.

They had stopped walking and were standing face to face in the middle of the living room. Maggie was studying the old braided carpet. She thought she recognized the fabric in the fifth row from the center—one of the wool shirts Lars had worn in the second grade. She stared at it for a long time. When she spoke her voice was soft. She lifted her eyes, studying the ceiling. "You said something while we were picking blackberries last summer," she said. "Something about truth— following after truth. Hounding it to death."

Mr. Engles nodded.

"How do you know? How do you know when you've come to the end? Hound it to death . . . to death. Isn't death the end?"

"Is it?"

Maggie shook her head.

Mr. Engles moved toward the couch and lowered himself slowly. "Isn't that exactly what the gospel of Jesus teaches us, Maggie? That death is not the end?"

Maggie didn't reply.

"The truth is there, Maggie, for those who seek it. God has promised us that." He patted the spot on the couch next to him. "Sit here," he said. "I want to read you something." He rose to get his old worn Bible. When he returned, Maggie was seated obediently on the couch. Mr. Engles leafed through the tissue-thin pages.

"Here," he said, "listen. 'Incline thine ear unto wisdom, and apply thine heart to understanding; yea, if thou criest after knowledge, and liftest up

thy voice for understanding; if thou seekest her as
silver, and searchest for her as for hid treasures;
then shalt thou understand the fear of the Lord,
and find the knowledge of God.' "

Maggie shook her head. "My questions aren't
like that," she said. "I'm not trying to understand
God—I don't even care about God. I just want to
know why—" She stopped and lowered her head.

Mr. Engles placed his hand on her knee.
"Maggie, I don't know what question you want
answered—I don't want to know, I'm too old to
know these things. But I suspect this surface
question, this thing you don't understand, has
colored your concept of God." Maggie pressed
her lips together. Mr. Engles took her hand in his.
"Maggie, God wants you to know him, understand
him. God is reasonable. He is just. If you will
follow the truth you have—follow it to the
end—he will give you more truth. He has promised."

Maggie rose to her feet again and began pacing
around the room.

*"I love you more than anything . . . except my
God."*

Suddenly she stopped her pacing. She whirled
on Mr. Engles, then folded her arms across her
chest. "But why? Why do I have to go scrounging
around for the answer? Why can't he just show
me—tell me?"

Mr. Engles shook his head and smiled a sad
smile. Then he looked straight into her blazing
eyes. "Because, Maggie," he said simply, "you
wouldn't believe him."

Maggie stared at him. The truth of his answer grazed her mind.

"Is it so hard, Maggie?"

She nodded her head.

"Do you know what it is you have to do?"

Again Maggie nodded.

Mr. Engles's voice was barely audible. "Then do it, Maggie. Do it."

Maggie stared into his eyes in silence. Finally she said, "May I use your telephone?"

"Of course."

She called Andrew. She told him she wouldn't be home till later.

19 REVELATIONS

Dr. Ralph Trimble was staying at the DeHaro Hotel, in the same room in which Maggie and Andrew had spent their wedding night—the Presidential Suite. It was called that because Teddy Roosevelt had stayed there while he was president. There was a huge painting of him in the lobby. When Maggie and Andrew were on their honeymoon they had stared at his signature in the guest book. But since then it had been stolen. Now there was just a note: "Teddy Roosevelt's signature used to be here."

Maggie climbed the narrow, creaky steps to the second story. The Presidential Suite was at the end of the hallway, and as Maggie walked toward it she realized again how uneven the floor was—it rose in the middle and then sloped down again toward the other end of the hall, as if sagging between the support timbers.

As Maggie knocked on the door she glanced at her watch. Eight-thirty. She hoped Dr. Trimble hadn't retired early. But in a moment the door was opened by a smiling Dr. Trimble. Before she could speak, he motioned her inside with an expansive gesture of his arms. "Come in, come in," he said.

Maggie blinked at him, befuddled by his robust manner and his apparent recognition of her. "I—I hope I'm not disturbing you," she said.

"No, no, Maggie, of course not," he said. "That is right, isn't it? Maggie?"

She nodded.

"I'm just doing some last-minute packing," he continued. "I'm taking the first ferry in the morning."

Maggie twisted her hands together. "Well, I won't keep you long," she said. "You'll need your rest."

Dr. Trimble waved her words aside. "Nonsense," he said. "We don't need half the sleep we think we do."

Maggie's first impulse was to correct him. *Speak for yourself.* Instead she nodded silently and stepped into the musty room.

Dr. Trimble closed the door behind her and then studied her face a moment. "You're lovely," he said. "No wonder Lars loved you."

Maggie stared at him.

At least she wasn't going to have to beat around the bush. But how could he speak so lightly of something that was so . . . so secret—so mixed up and confusing?

She glanced around the room uneasily before

sitting on the red velvet settee he offered her. There was a fire going in the fireplace and Maggie, shivering with nervousness, was grateful for its warmth. As Dr. Trimble pulled a heavy antique chair closer to the settee, she continued to study the room.

She remembered the wallpaper. Row after row of wild flowers—tiny bouquets of wild flowers. They had reminded her of the bouquet she had gathered on the cape. She had lain in bed on her honeymoon and counted them. There were thirty-four bouquets in the row next to the ceiling on the wall opposite the bed.

Dr. Trimble settled in the old chair and said, "What can I do for you, Maggie?" His voice was loud and deep. He had altered his pulpit voice only a trifle. Maggie was sure his words could be heard next door.

"You . . . you know about me," Maggie began. Her words were not exactly a question, but not a statement either. Dr. Trimble nodded his head. His face was solemn. Maggie bit her lip. "I . . . I've hated you for so long . . . it's hard not to start there."

"That's as good a place as any," he said. His voice had softened.

"I . . . I don't know." She rose from the chair and walked to the window. She stared at the harbor, the same harbor she had stared at on her wedding night. Narrow creases formed lines across her brow as she turned to face Dr. Trimble. "I just need to know some things," she said. She rubbed her forehead. "I've tried to figure it out but," she brushed her hand through the air, "I can't."

Maggie returned to the chair and stood behind it, gripping the back of it with tense fingers. "I thought . . . well, I thought the journal, Lars's prayer journal might help. If I could just borrow it—even for one night, since you're leaving right away. I . . . I'd get it back to you before you leave in the morning." She held one arm in the air, her fist tightly clenched. "If I could just understand this thing . . . this thing between God and Lars, maybe I could understand . . . I don't know . . . some of the other things."

Dr. Trimble was still. When he spoke his voice was gentle. "What things, Maggie?"

Maggie stared at him. She didn't want to put it into words—trivialize it by exposing it to his scorn. Just another broken romance. He must have heard a thousand stories like hers over the years. Probably had a canned sermon ready and waiting. But she'd come this far.

She took a deep breath and gripped the chair with both hands. "Why," she said, gripping her fingers tighter on the chair back, ". . . why he broke up with me." The veins in her hands were standing out in blue ridges.

Dr. Trimble rose to his feet. It was his turn to walk to the window and stare at the harbor. He kept his back to her as he spoke. "Why do you think?" he asked.

Some of his force was gone, his assurance. Maggie let go of the chair and walked to his side. She looked at him as she spoke, but he continued to stare out the window. "You said . . . you said that there was a double standard . . . boys wouldn't accept in girls what they would accept in. . . ."

"That's not *always* true—that wasn't it."

"What then—what?"

"Lars didn't explain to you?"

Maggie shook her head. "He wouldn't see me. He wrote me a note but I—"

Dr. Trimble pushed his chin forward and peered at her. "You what?"

"I . . . I sent it back. I was too angry to read it."

Dr. Trimble pulled back his chin and stroked it. He turned to the window again. "Why did you come here tonight, Maggie? Just to find out about Lars?"

Maggie thought for a moment and then began pacing around the tiny room. She stopped behind the chair and rested her hands on it. "I hate God," she said quietly. "Mr. Engles said that if I hate God it's because I don't know him—that I don't know the truth about him. All I know," Maggie said, gripping the chair fiercely, "is that Lars and I were committed to each other—before God we were committed to each other. And that same God, the God we asked to cement our vows. . . ." Her eyes were blazing and the veins in her neck were standing out. "That same God took him away from me."

Dr. Trimble turned around. "Vows? What vows?" he demanded.

His vehemence startled Maggie, robbing her of her anger. "On the cape," she said. "We had a little wedding, just Lars, me, and God." She let her hand fall through the air. "We had a little pretend wedding with grass rings."

Dr. Trimble stared at her in silence. Then he walked over to the dresser and opened up the top drawer. He lifted out several dog-eared spiral notebooks and a number of hard-covered book-keeping ledgers. Dr. Trimble leafed through the top journal intensely, not looking at the words, but sifting through the pages as if searching for something. "There it is," he said. He turned to Maggie. "Does this mean anything to you?"

Maggie stared at the open journal. The page was lined and columned, but covered with Lars's squared-off handwriting, the faint, vertical red lines barely visible beneath his broad black lettering. Maggie caught a word here and there as she scanned the page, but then she noticed what Dr. Trimble was pointing to. There, almost lost in the crease in the center, pressed and flat, was a tiny dried grass ring. It was brown and fragile, but Maggie would have recognized it anywhere.

She lowered herself onto the chair and reached for the journal. Dr. Trimble gave it to her and she rested it on her knees. She stared at the ring and then touched it with her fingertip. "All these years," she whispered.

Dr. Trimble sat down on the bed. "Maggie, I want you to have the journals. To keep. Samantha gave them to me—they were among Lars's things. She said I could . . . well, she thought you might like to have them. I wasn't sure, but . . . I think she's right. I think you should have them."

Maggie's eyes filled with tears. "But surely Samantha wants them," she said. "They were engaged. Surely. . . ."

He raised his hand to silence her. "I know they were engaged," he said. He studied Maggie solemnly. When he spoke his voice was quiet, reverent almost. "But you and Lars were married."

Maggie let out a silent gasp and leaned forward, staring into the holy face of Dr. Ralph Trimble, her eyes asking the question for which she'd given up ever having an answer. "Were we?" she whispered.

Dr. Trimble leaned forward and took Maggie's hand. His eyes were shiny as he looked into Maggie's haunted face—the same haunted look he'd seen so often in Lars's eyes.

He nodded his head slowly. "I think so," he said. "In a way. You had a partial marriage at least. Lars never forgot his vows to you, Maggie, he never did. I didn't know about your ceremony up on the cape. Lars never told me. But I always knew there was something . . . something important he couldn't share."

Something gave way inside of Maggie—a sinking and tossing of her emotions. Her face crumbled and her shoulders began to shake. She sobbed quietly for several moments. Dr. Trimble gave her his handkerchief.

When she had dried her eyes he handed her the rest of the journals. "Read these, Maggie. Read them. You will learn about God—the true God—Lars's God."

20 THE JOURNALS

When Maggie arrived home the house was dark.
Andrew and Rachel had gone to bed. Maggie
switched on the living room light and caught her
breath. She'd forgotten about Peter and Annie—
they were asleep on the living room floor. They
were sprawled on their backs, their faces relaxed
and innocent. One of Annie's arms was crossed
over Peter's and Peter had squirmed nearly out of
his sleeping bag.

The light hadn't wakened them, so Maggie left
it on. She didn't want to go into the bedroom. If
someone woke up, better the children than
Andrew. She put the journals on the couch and
then adjusted Peter's sleeping bag to cover him
better. Then she went into the kitchen to heat
some water.

A few minutes later she settled on the couch
with the journals and a cup of hot tea. She
glanced through the journals, checking to see

which were the oldest. They were all dated, and when she found the earliest one she realized Lars had started keeping his prayer journal that long-ago November—right after Spiritual Emphasis Week. She held the closed journal on her lap and relived for a moment the crisp fall days— leaves littering the campus and posters appearing everywhere. "Dr. Ralph Trimble—Prepare for a Blessing."

Maggie took a deep breath and opened the first spiral notebook. She took a sip of her tea and then paused to remove an envelope stuck between the pages. She pulled it out, intending to use it later as a bookmark. But it was quite thick, and then the letters on the front caught her attention. She stared at them and gasped.

"Margaret," it said, in half-block letters, faded with age.

". . . *Lars asked me to give you this.*"

Maggie stared at the envelope in her hand. Stared and stared at it. How many times had she wondered what it had contained?

"He can keep his little notes and his little God all to himself." How many times had she regretted her impulsive refusal to read it?

"Hound it to death, Maggie. Hound it to death."

She fingered the envelope lightly, almost playfully, and lifted her eyes to the ceiling. "Oh, Lars . . ." she whispered, "still passing notes." Then she smiled weakly, as if she had met his sparkling eyes and they once again shared a little joke.

Maggie examined the envelope with her

fingers. It was thick. It would take a while to read. That was good. With trembling fingers she opened the envelope and began.

Dear Maggie,

When I saw you at the foot of the stairs— saw the look on your face—I was convinced there was no way to make you understand.

But I have to try.

Some of the things I want to explain are things that have been bugging me for a long time—but I could never quite get them into words. I'm still not sure I can, but I'll try.

I love you, Maggie, I love you more than anything in the world. And I want to marry you, in a church, with witnesses and with everyone's blessing. But before we can get married I need to get some things straightened around in my head.

You have been my idol. I have put you before everything—before God.

I've always wanted to talk to you about our wedding . . . you know . . . at the top of the cape. I meant those vows. I mean, I really meant them, and I intend to live them out. But for some reason it's hard for me to talk about it.

I've thought a lot about our private cere- mony and why, when we meant what we said, I still feel guilty about our relationship. No matter what I tell myself, that little ceremony doesn't seem to count. It counts, our words count, the promises we made to each other count, but somehow that ceremony doesn't

give us license to do the things we've been
doing. Because, Maggie, I know, and I think
you know too that we were just trying to use
that little ceremony to make ourselves feel
better about . . . about—you know.

Marriage is more than that. You were right,
Maggie. Up on the cape when I asked you
what it meant to be married you said it
meant having babies and staying together in
sickness and in health.

All of that, you said.

All of that.

And you were right. I tried to narrow it
down to just being committed to each other—
sexually committed—promising that we
would be faithful to each other. But that's not
what marriage is. That's part of it—a large
part—but that's not all of it. A marriage is
when two people live together—make a life
together. That means providing for each other,
helping each other, creating a home. We're not
willing to do that yet. We want to finish
school. "Therefore shall a man leave his father
and his mother and shall cleave unto his wife;
and they shall be one flesh." We're not ready
for all of what that means.

And there's something else. We could walk
away from each other today and nobody
would be there to encourage us to follow
through on our commitment—because
nobody knows anything about it. There's
something important about that, Maggie,
about admitting we need others to help us live
out our commitment to each other. It has to do

with pride and arrogance—thinking we can do it on our own. I was so sure of my ability to love and be faithful to you, and I was so sure of your ability to love and be faithful to me, that I put all my faith in that, instead of in God, trusting him enough to obey him. We need God and other people to help us follow through on our feeble commitments. But we didn't admit that.

We will need help to live out our commitment to each other. I guess that's why marriages are public—ceremonies with witnesses. Dr. Trimble says it is hard enough within marriage to follow through on commitments, but at least when we are feeling weak we have something to prod us and encourage us. Outside of marriage we have no support system.

Does any of this make sense to you? You probably think I'm nuts.

Maggie, I told Dr. Trimble about us. He says we need time away from each other. I need time to straighten out my relationship with God.

I love you, Maggie. I will love you forever. But I have loved you more than God himself. And that is what I must get squared away before we can renew our relationship. I know we can have a wonderful life together. Please be patient with me.

Maggie, I'm sorry I can't tell you these things in person—but I can't. I've tried, even before I talked to Dr. Trimble—way last summer—but I just could never get the words out. When I'm with you it doesn't seem important. But it is important. You've always understood me, Maggie. More than anyone else. Please try to understand me now.

Forgive me. Forgive me for wanting you too much—for all the guilt and pain I've caused you. The misunderstanding. Your face looking up the stairs at me—so hurt and betrayed.

Please don't try to contact me again. I don't think I can stand it. Perhaps in a few months. . . .

Will you ever forgive me?

Lars

Maggie closed her eyes and sat in silence for a long while. She turned the envelope over in her hand. *Margaret*, it said, in faded squarish letters.

"I love you more than anything . . . except my God."

"Hound it to death, Maggie. Make sense of it."

For a moment she could feel the cold metal of that bathroom stall against her back and she could remember feeling so guilty and abandoned. So sure that Lars and God—self-righteous and secure in the maleness of their double-standard world—had betrayed her. So angry.

Why had she been so impulsive? Why couldn't she have trusted him more—at least have read his letter? If she couldn't trust Lars, she could at least have trusted God.

Annie whimpered. In his sleep Peter had flung his arm across her face. Maggie set the journals aside and knelt on the floor beside the children. She untangled their arms and legs and tucked their limp bodies more securely into the sleeping bags. As she studied Annie's pixie-sweet face, she remembered the day she'd hung over Annie's crib, a blood-stained sheet stuffed between her legs. So long ago. Just a nightmare.

But down the hall, asleep in their double bed, was Andrew, a crushed, silent reminder of what she'd done. Maggie sighed, then glanced at her watch.

She rose from her knees and returned to the kitchen for another cup of tea. There was a bowl of leftover popcorn on the counter. It was stale, but she took it back into the living room with her. Maggie sat back down on the couch and nibbled on the mushy popcorn. She let her eyes rest on the journals, but did not pick them up. She was anxious to read them, but did not want to begin. Starting to read them was like being born—the beginning of death. The sooner she began, the sooner she would be finished. She never wanted to finish. She wanted to live inside of them forever.

Maggie's tea got cold. But she sipped it slowly as she finished eating the popcorn. At last she picked up the earliest spiral notebook. She studied the familiar handwriting a moment, squarish, half print, half script. She loved it so much.

She began to read.

It was an outpouring of anguish, written shortly after they'd broken up. "I know I promised you, God, but I love her so much. She won't understand. She'll hate me. . . . She's gone. She left. Oh, God, what—what are you trying to do to me? It's something like Abraham offering up Isaac. He didn't actually have to do it, but he had to be willing to do it. Sometimes I think I've got it turned around—I'm having to do it, but I'm still not willing."

Maggie read on and on. Her tea was completely cold by now, but she sipped at it anyway. Shortly after she had married Andrew: "Maybe I'm nuts. Maybe we're all nuts—all of us who think we're talking to you—think we understand you and know what you want us to do."

Maggie leaned her head back and closed her eyes. Lars had felt cheated too. Thought God had double-crossed him. "God . . . oh, my God. She married Andrew. How could you let her do that? Maybe I was wrong to break up with her. Maybe I should have done what I wanted to do instead. Maybe that's the only thing worth obeying—my own desires."

Gradually the tenor of his prayers began to change. The anguish was still there, but Lars began to write of other things—his schoolwork, his future. He wrote of people in faraway lands who knew nothing about God.

And then there was one entry just before he left for Ecuador: "Father, I've been blaming you for a lot of things that aren't your fault. Maggie and I got ourselves into our predicament by not obeying you in the first place. I'm still not sure I did the right thing by breaking up with her—at least not the way I went about it—but, Father, I really thought I was obeying you. What must Maggie think? Does she hate me? You? Dear Father, please show her, please, please show her that you love her. Lord, if I should go to Ecuador and pour out my life for those there who don't know you, but then Maggie . . . Maggie is lost to you, I would feel—I would feel my life wasted. Love her, Father."

Maggie wept softly. She read page after page. And she could sense Lars's faith growing. While she had been cramming her anger inside where it had fermented and become rancid, Lars had been confessing his to God. And in the process God had been washing him clean.

Mr. Engles was right. The God she had hated all these years was not the true God. The true God was the one Lars worshiped—the one he dared to bare his soul to—confident that he was loved and forgiven. It was the God she had worshiped as a child—the ruler of her magic kingdom.

A much later entry: "Father, I've been thinking about that verse again—'The grass withereth, the flower fadeth . . . but the word of the Lord abideth forever.' Thinking about Maggie, our vows at the top of the cape. I suppose all these years—never marrying—I've been trying to live up to those vows. But it's not possible, is it? There's really no meaningful way I can live up to the things I promised Maggie. I confess that to you, Father. I confess my inability to live up to my own words. Please forgive me, Father—both for the arrogance with which I made them, and for all the hurt I caused her.

" 'The grass withereth'—oh, God. Help me to forgive myself for being a part of that—a part of all that is fading and withering. Help me to see myself cleansed and renewed—recreated in your image, conformed unto your Son."

Later there was an entry mentioning Samantha. "She's a lovely woman, gentle, willing to wait upon you. Father . . . for the first time I am daring to think of marriage. I am trusting you for a new life, but . . . Maggie."

One of the final entries was made shortly after his mother's funeral. "Seeing Maggie again—how I dreaded and longed for it. I can never stop loving her, Father. I'm not going to try. But she is lost to me. I cannot reach her. I leave her to you, Father. I finally do, really, leave her to you. Love her."

The entries after that were brief and scattered. He mentioned Samantha often. Then his illness. His handwriting lost its squareness. As he grew weaker the letters became round and run together.

His last entry was a quote from one of the Psalms: " 'Precious in the sight of the Lord is the death of his saints.' What does that mean, Lord? That you don't take our deaths lightly—or that you look forward to them? I hope you look forward to them."

And his final words, "Remember Maggie."

Maggie sat silently for several moments, then gently closed the cover of his last journal.

"Remember Maggie."

She bowed her head, and in a moment tears began streaming down her cheeks, washing across her face—a shimmering veil of repentance. She wept for all her years of bitterness, sobbing quietly until the hardness inside began to soften and dissolve. She wept for Lars and all the anguish she had caused him. And she wept for Andrew—Andrew whose only sin was loving her. Then she hunched over, pulling her knees up to her breasts, and she sobbed for all her unborn children. Cried and cried. She could see the old prophet in his long white robe wagging his finger at her. She could see his face now. Sad. Not angry as she had thought. "This child shall die," he reminded her, "die before it is conceived, killed by your own bitterness and fear." He was sad, not angry. Her tears continued to flow, a mad release of her pent-up emotion, a thousand little pockets of fear and anger bursting as truth and joy pressed against them. It was as if her tears were springs of living water—their source God himself—washing her clean and free.

She squeezed her eyes together. "Father God," she said, "thank you. Thank you for loving me."

"If thou . . . liftest up thy voice for understanding . . . then shalt thou understand the fear of the Lord, and find the knowledge of God."

"Hound it to death."

"Isn't death the end?"

"Is it?"

It seemed to her that Lars had reached out to her from the grave—a picture of the resurrection. Buried . . . raised . . . and appearing to those who loved him. How grateful they must have been. She hugged the journals to herself. "Forgive me, God, for not trusting you—forgive me for hating you all these years. It just . . . it just hurt so much." She pressed the journals against her breast. "Thank you," she whispered. "Thank you for these. Thank you."

21 TRACES OF LIGHT

By the time Maggie slipped into bed beside Andrew, there were faint traces of morning streaking across the sky. Her stomach felt hollow and her head felt light—from sleeplessness and late-night hunger. But she had barely closed her eyes before she fell into a deep, dreamless sleep.

She was sleeping too soundly to notice when Andrew got up in the morning. But about ten o'clock she was awakened by Peter's and Annie's aborted attempts at silence. She heard the refrigerator door opening and closing and at one point some silverware clattering to the floor. She was aware of Rachel talking to the children in whispers and of their unsuccessful attempts to whisper back. Their voices were as loud as ever—perhaps even louder—but they had a forced, nasal quality.

"Shh," from Rachel.

"Good morning," Maggie called, to let them

know she was awake. Then she turned over, facing Andrew's side of the bed. Had he heard her come to bed? Probably not. A sound sleeper. Even during the nightmare years he'd slept through the night, oblivious to her tortured pacing.

She glanced at Lars's journals stacked next to the bed. It was a good thing she'd brought them in here. Rachel would surely have noticed them if she'd left them on the couch.

But what had she done with Lars's letter? She thought she'd left it on top. She couldn't remember. So sleepy. Probably tucked it inside one of the journals.

Rachel came to her door and peeked in. "We were trying not to waken you," she said.

Maggie smiled. "I know. I heard you."

Rachel shrugged her shoulders in helplessness as she watched Maggie swing her legs over the side of the bed and slip on her robe. "Coffee," Maggie muttered.

"It's all ready," Rachel replied cheerfully. "What time did you get home last night, anyway? I was trying to wait up for you but I couldn't keep my eyes open."

Maggie ran her fingers through her tangled hair as she followed Rachel into the kitchen. She plopped onto one of the kitchen chairs and took the cup of coffee Rachel handed her. "I don't know, about eleven o'clock, I guess." She yawned. The time when she got to sleep was the real issue.

"Was Mr. Engles OK?"

"Huh? Oh, yes. He was all right. But very lonely. He had started sorting through Lars's things and hadn't realized it would be so painful. I'm glad I stopped by. He . . . he needed someone."

Rachel sensed there was more. Something on Maggie's mind. But she didn't press. She always felt that way about Maggie. And no amount of probing made any difference. "Well," Rachel said, "I was hoping to catch the eleven o'clock ferry. I'd better hustle."

"Goodness," Maggie said, rising abruptly. "I'd better fix you some breakfast."

Rachel laughed. "You're a little late," she said. "We had cereal."

Maggie leaned her elbow on the counter and waved her other arm through the air. "You must be overwhelmed by my hospitality," she said, "taking off last night—leaving you to fix your own breakfast. . . ."

"We're family, Maggie," Rachel said, heading toward the living room to roll up the children's sleeping bags.

"It's a good thing," Maggie muttered as she followed her.

Together they managed to get Rachel's things packed and ready to go. Peter and Annie were dancing around in excitement—as eager to leave as they'd been to come.

Even though it was cold, Maggie decided to walk to the ferry with them. They walked quickly, partly because they feared being late and partly to help keep themselves warm. But as they reached the shore they could see the ferry hadn't even docked yet. It was gliding silently through the water toward them.

"I'm kind of surprised Andrew didn't come

down to see you off," Maggie said, "—the kids especially."

Rachel frowned. "He came in early and said good-bye," she replied. She paused. "Is he all right? He seems kind of ... I don't know ... down."

They had stopped walking and were leaning against the rail close to the dock. Maggie watched the ferry pull up to the dock. Car engines started. The chain at the mouth of the ferry was lowered, and one by one the cars drove across the clackety ramp onto the island.

Maggie chewed on her lower lip a moment, then suddenly turned back to Rachel. "I told him about the operation," she said. "Last week."

Rachel stepped forward in surprise and touched her arm. "Oh, my ... is he ... ?"

Maggie shrugged her shoulders. "I don't know. We haven't talked. Lars died. . . ." She let her arm fall through the air. "We just haven't talked."

The last of the cars drove onto the island and the outgoing passengers began to get on board. Maggie picked up one of Rachel's bags and handed it to her. Rachel called the children. They were a few feet away, throwing pebbles into the water. Rachel placed her hand on Maggie's shoulder. "Maggie, I don't think you've ever realized how much Andrew loves you. You could never do anything to make him stop loving you."

Maggie bit her lip and shook her head slowly from side to side. "I certainly don't deserve it," she said. But Rachel didn't hear her. She had turned toward the children—was trying to herd them onto the boat. She turned back to Maggie.

"Give him a little time," she said. "He'll be all right." She was moving toward the ferry. "But take better care of him, will you?" she called over her shoulder. "He's the only brother I have."

"I'll try," Maggie hollered. " 'Bye, Annie! 'Bye, Peter! Good-bye, Rachel. Thanks."

As Maggie walked back to the house she glanced at her watch. Andrew only worked till noon on Saturday. He would be home soon. She dreaded seeing him.

When she got back home she was at loose ends. She didn't feel like cleaning house—her usual Saturday chore—but she didn't feel like doing anything else either. She went into the bedroom and knelt beside the stack of journals and pondered what to do with them. Put them in the back of the linen closet, she supposed. But what had she done with the letter?

The telephone rang. She hurried into the kitchen to answer it. It was Andrew's father, wanting to talk to Andrew.

"He's not here," Maggie said.

Strange. She'd assumed Andrew was working at his father's.

"Probably down at the ferry seeing off Rachel and those kids, huh? He's sure crazy about those kids."

Maggie's mind was racing. The kids?
"Oh . . . yes. Yes, he is. He's crazy about them. They took the eleven o'clock ferry. I . . . I'm sure he'll be home soon. Can I give him a message?"

"Not really. I just wondered when he planned to finish up the reports for the Agriculture Department. No hurry. I was just kind of surprised when he didn't show for work this morning. He didn't say anything last night. You can usually set your watch by him, you know."

"I know—well, listen . . . I'll tell him you called. You're sure it's nothing urgent?"

"No, no. Just a little surprised is all."

After Maggie hung up the phone she stared out the kitchen window for several moments. Then she returned to the bedroom. She really was sure she'd left the letter on top. She thumbed through several of the journals. It wasn't there. She went into the living room and checked behind the cushions on the couch. Not there.

"You can usually set your watch by him, you know."

Maggie ran her fingers through her hair. Where was he? She hadn't explained where she was going last night—only that she'd be home late. Andrew wasn't a curious man by nature. But the journals had been right there beside the bed—the letter on top. She could see it there, the way she'd left it last night—a yellowed rectangular envelope with the word "Margaret" on the front, in squarish letters.

Surely Andrew wouldn't have taken it. Out of character. . . . *"You could usually set your watch by him."* Matchbox cars scattered across the floor in Winter Fantasyland. Tonka trucks crashing after them.

Maggie began pacing back and forth across the bedroom. She tried to remember what the letter said. How would it sound to Andrew?

"Private ceremony . . . trying to make ourselves feel better about . . . about—you know."

She ran her fingers through her hair again and again.

"You could never do anything to make him stop loving you."

Maggie shook her head. Where was he? Why hadn't he gone to work? Why didn't he come home?

It was a new experience—not knowing where Andrew was. Suddenly it seemed important to her. That knowing. That security of knowing.

She paced around the house for over an hour. Andrew didn't return. Finally, unable to stand the empty house another moment, she donned her yellow rain slicker and headed for the beach.

Out of habit, she headed for the old barnacle-covered boulder. She didn't go directly to it, but sat on a driftwood log close by. She forced her eyes across the gray horizon before allowing them to rest on the old rock and its stubborn company of fortressed sea creatures.

"They're safe, I suppose, but it sounds pretty dull to me. Don't you agree, Margaret?"

"It sounds rather nice."

What if Andrew hadn't been there when she'd come home from college, so distraught and lonely? He'd never asked any questions. Just wanted her to marry him. She held her head between her hands. She supposed she loved him—in a way. Needed him. Needed him for sure.

Where could he be? Andrew didn't have any favorite haunts—no special places.

Where would he go?

The ruins? Even Lars was afraid to go down there.

She stared at the sea and the sky, the rocks and the sand.

A place where Lars had never been.

Maggie tossed the stick aside and hurried toward the house.

She drove to the north end of the island, toward the mausoleum and the old McMillin ruins. When she got to Roche Harbor she spotted Andrew's pickup parked at the foot of the trail leading to the mausoleum. She parked her car behind it and then hurried up the trail through the cold, wet woods. When she got to the mausoleum she found it deserted. The trail down the other side of the hill to the ruins was narrower and steeper, but Maggie hurried through the woods, ignoring the wet branches slapping across her cheeks.

The trail ended on another road, and across the road she could see the ivy-covered ruins. Then she saw Andrew, leaning against one of the stone chimneys. She didn't call out to him, but he noticed her as she was crossing the road.

She walked to the edge of the ruins, then stopped. They stared at each other in silence. Finally Maggie said, "Your dad called. Wondered why you hadn't shown up for work."

Andrew didn't say anything.

"Have you been here all morning?"

He still didn't speak.

"Andrew," she said, "I . . . I've been worried about you." She was surprised by the truth of her words.

He stared across the ruins into the distance.

"Did . . . did you read Lars's letter?"

She could see the muscles tense in his neck and across his cheeks. Finally he nodded his head. It was a tiny movement, but a movement, nevertheless.

"I'm sorry, Andrew, I. . . ."

"You always loved him, didn't you?"

She walked slowly toward him.

Andrew turned away from her and leaned against the ancient ivy-covered chimney. "Like I loved you," he said, "always. All the years we were growing up together you only had eyes for Lars. You wanted to play the games Lars wanted to play. Lars was the only one who mattered." He stared toward the bay hidden behind the trees. "Do you know what I've been thinking about all morning?" He turned to look at her. She closed her eyes. She didn't want to hear it. *Tramp. Slut.* She shook her head.

"I've been thinking about your father."

She looked up, surprised. "My father?"

"About his promise to you."

Maggie stared at him. He had been stumbling around these ruins all morning thinking about her father's promise? She remembered the day Andrew had found her working on her path. *Didn't balance, huh?*. . . trying to understand her, always trying to get inside of her and piece things together. Had he spent as much time trying to figure her out as she'd spent trying to understand Lars and God?

"You told me about it when we were up here before, remember? Right after you came back from Seattle."

Maggie lowered her chin and nodded.

"He promised to come back. And Lars too. He couldn't keep his promises either. Partly," Andrew said, pressing his fist against the old stone chimney, "partly because of me. I rushed in and married you when . . . when I knew you really weren't ready."

He turned to her and his eyes were red-rimmed, tiny lines creasing outward from the corners. "I just . . . I just loved you so much. You came home from college angry at Lars, never wanting to see him again, and I could see you'd been hurt—terribly, terribly hurt." He paused, staring across the ruins. "But I was more interested in getting what I wanted than I was in giving you time to heal." He rubbed his thumb against his lower lip. "I knew you loved him . . . I guess I always knew that . . . but I didn't care, I figured in time you would learn to love me—I would make you love me. I just barged right in and blew everything to pieces."

Maggie shook her head. "You didn't blow it, Andrew. We did—Lars and I. He was the only thing in the world that mattered to me. I never should have married you—not when I did—it wasn't fair. There were too many things unresolved, too many things I didn't understand. But, now . . . well, now so many things have changed. Maybe now we could start over—have a marriage—a real marriage."

Maggie looked deeply into Andrew's eyes, but he looked away again, focusing his attention into the distance, "Why?" he asked, bitterness edging his voice. "Because now he's dead? Now you know for sure you can't have him?"

Maggie bit her lip and studied his pain-filled face. "Andrew, listen," she said. "I suppose Lars's death makes a difference—perhaps it should make a difference, but that's not the important thing. The important thing is that now I understand it." She looked into his face earnestly. "I could never finish it before. Because it didn't make sense. Lars didn't make sense—and God didn't make sense."

She took a step toward him. "I haven't kept my promises, Andrew, not to God, not to Lars—not to you. I haven't been any kind of wife to you, Andrew. I . . . in my heart I was still married to Lars." She waved her hand through the air. "Well, not married, I guess. We weren't married . . . at least not in a way that really counted."

Andrew shoved his hands into his pockets and lifted his clouded forehead toward the gray sky. "Oh, it counted," he whispered.

Maggie stared at him a moment. Then she nodded her head. "Maybe it did," she said. "But it's as if I've had part of a marriage in this hand and part in the other." She brought her hands together. "If I could have brought them together in one relationship . . . but as it was. . . ."

Andrew lowered his head.

Maggie stepped to his side and touched his arm. "Andrew, you have been wonderful to me—far beyond what I deserve. I don't know what I'd have done. . . ." She lowered her head. When she looked back into his face, her eyes were shining with a white, bright light. "Andrew," she said, gripping his arm with her fingers, leaning toward him, her body tense and expectant, ". . . on the ferry, on our way back from Seattle, I was staring at the water, and I was all alone, and the water was bright and shining and burning into my eyes and. . . ." She let go of his sleeve and folded her arms close to her body, digging her fingernails into her upper arms until she could feel the sharpness of her nails through her wool jacket. She felt the hotness behind her eyes and blinked to hold back her tears. "And I . . . I was so afraid . . . so afraid of losing you."

She gazed into his face, the white, shiny light in her eyes burning into his. "I love you, Andrew. I do. It's an imperfect, mixed up love, like our crazy mixed up marriage, but it exists. It *is.* "

She touched his arms, "Andrew, we have made promises to each other." She squeezed her fingers into the sleeve of his jacket. "We have vowed to stay together and love each other for better or for worse. For once in my life—just once—I'd like to live out the promises I've made." She looked into his eyes. "I'm asking you to forgive me—to give me a chance to be a real wife to you."

Andrew leaned his shoulder against the chimney and stared into the distance. "I'm afraid to commit myself to you again, Maggie. What if I can't. . . . I wanted a family—I still do. What if, in the end, I find I can't forgive you? I . . . I don't want to be just one more person making promises that can't be kept."

Maggie looked into his face. "You've already made them, Andrew." She stepped away from him and faced him squarely. "That's just it, Andrew,

Other Living Books Bestsellers

THE BEST CHRISTMAS PAGEANT EVER by Barbara Robinson. A delightfully wild and funny story about what can happen to a Christmas program when the "horrible Herdman" family of brothers and sisters are miscast in the roles of the Christmas story characters from the Bible. 07–0137 $2.50.

ELIJAH by William H. Stephens. He was a rough-hewn farmer who strolled onto the stage of history to deliver warnings to Ahab the king and to defy Jezebel the queen. A powerful biblical novel you will never forget. 07–4023 $3.95.

THE TOTAL MAN by Dan Benson. A practical guide on how to gain confidence and fulfillment. Covering areas such as budgeting of time, money matters, and marital relationships. 07–7289 $3.50.

HOW TO HAVE ALL THE TIME YOU NEED EVERY DAY by Pat King. Drawing from her own and other women's experiences as well as from the Bible and the research of time experts, Pat has written a warm and personal book for every Christian woman. 07–1529 $3.50.

IT'S INCREDIBLE by Ann Kiemel. "It's incredible" is what some people say when a slim young woman says, "Hi, I'm Ann," and starts talking about love and good and beauty. As Ann tells about a Jesus who can make all the difference in their lives, some call that incredible, and turn away. Others become miracles themselves, agreeing with Ann that it's incredible. 07–1818 $2.50.

THE PEPPERMINT GANG AND THE EVERGEEN CASTLE by Laurie Clifford. A heartwarming story about the growing pains of five children whose hilarious adventures teach them unforgettable lessons about love and forgiveness, life and death. Delightful reading for all ages. 07–0779 $3.50.

JOHN, SON OF THUNDER by Ellen Gunderson Traylor. Travel with John down the desert paths, through the courts of the Holy City, and to the foot of the cross. Journey with him from his luxury as a privileged son of Israel to the bitter hardship of his exile on Patmos. This is a saga of adventure, romance, and discovery—of a man bigger than life—the disciple "whom Jesus loved." 07–1903 $3.95.

WHAT'S IN A NAME? compiled by Linda Francis, John Hartzel, and Al Palmquist. A fascinating name dictionary that features the literal meaning of people's first names, the character quality implied by the name, and an applicable Scripture verse for each name listed. Ideal for expectant parents! 07–7935 $2.95.

Other Living Books Bestsellers

THE MAN WHO COULD DO NO WRONG by Charles E. Blair with John and Elizabeth Sherrill. He built one of the largest churches in America . . . then he made a mistake. This is the incredible story of Pastor Charles E. Blair, accused of massive fraud. A book "for error-prone people in search of the Christian's secret for handling mistakes." 07–4002 $3.50.

GIVERS, TAKERS AND OTHER KINDS OF LOVERS by Josh McDowell. This book bypasses vague generalities about love and sex and gets right down to basic questions: Whatever happened to sexual freedom? What's true love like? What is your most important sex organ? Do men respond differently than women? If you're looking for straight answers about God's plan for love and sexuality then this book was written for you. 07–1031 $2.50.

MORE THAN A CARPENTER by Josh McDowell. This best selling author thought Christians must be "out of their minds." He put them down. He argued against their faith. But eventually he saw that his arguments wouldn't stand up. In this book, Josh focuses upon the person who changed his life—Jesus Christ. 07–4552 $2.50.

HIND'S FEET ON HIGH PLACES by Hannah Hurnard. A classic allegory which has sold more than a million copies! 07–1429 $3.50.

THE CATCH ME KILLER by Bob Erler with John Souter. Golden gloves, black bell, green beret, silver badge. Supercop Bob Erler had earned the colors of manhood. Now can he survive prison life? An incredible true story of forgiveness and hope. 07–0214 $3.50.

WHAT WIVES WISH THEIR HUSBANDS KNEW ABOUT WOMEN by Dr. James Dobson. By the best selling author of *DARE TO DISCIPLINE* and *THE STRONG-WILLED CHILD,* here's a vital book that speaks to the unique emotional needs and aspirations of today's woman. An immensely practical, interesting guide. 07–7896 $2.95.

PONTIUS PILATE by Dr. Paul Maier. This fascinating novel is about one of the most famous Romans in history—the man who declared Jesus innocent but who nevertheless sent him to the cross. This powerful biblical novel gives you a unique insight into the life and death of Jesus. 07–4852 $3.95.

LIFE IS TREMENDOUS by Charlie Jones. Believing that enthusiasm makes the difference, Jones shows how anyone can be happy, involved, relevant, productive, healthy, and secure in the midst of a high-pressure, commercialized, automated society. 07–2184 $2.50.

HOW TO BE HAPPY THOUGH MARRIED by Dr. Tim LaHaye. One of America's most successful marriage counselors gives practical, proven advice for marital happiness. 07–1499 $2.95.

Other Living Books Bestsellers

DAVID AND BATHSHEBA by Roberta Kells Dorr. Was Bathsheba an innocent country girl or a scheming adulteress? What was King David really like? Solomon—the wisest man in the world—was to be king, but could he survive his brothers' intrigues? Here is an epic love story which comes radiantly alive through the art of a fine storyteller. 07–0618 $4.50.

TOO MEAN TO DIE by Nick Pirovolos with William Proctor. In this action-packed story, Nick the Greek tells how he grew from a scrappy immigrant boy to a fearless underworld criminal. Finally caught, he was imprisoned. But something remarkable happened and he was set free—truly set free! 07–7283 $3.95.

FOR WOMEN ONLY. This bestseller gives a balanced, entertaining, diversified treatment of all aspects of womanhood. Edited by Evelyn and J. Allan Petersen, founder of Family Concern. 07–0897 $3.95.

FOR MEN ONLY. Edited by J. Allan Petersen, this book gives solid advice on how men can cope with the tremendous pressures they face every day as fathers, husbands, workers. 07–0892 $3.50.

ROCK. What is rock music really doing to you? Bob Larson presents a well-researched and penetrating look at today's rock music and rock performers. What are lyrics really saying? Who are the top performers and what are their life-styles? 07–5686 $2.95.

THE ALCOHOL TRAP by Fred Foster. A successful film executive was about to lose everything—his family's vacation home, his house in New Jersey, his reputation in the film industry, his wife. This is an emotion-packed story of hope and encouragement, offering valuable insights into the troubled world of high pressure living and alcoholism. 07–0078 $2.95.

LET ME BE A WOMAN. Best selling author Elisabeth Elliot (author of *THROUGH GATES OF SPLENDOR*) presents her profound and unique perspective on womanhood. This is a significant book on a continuing controversial subject. 07–2162 $3.50.

WE'RE IN THE ARMY NOW by Imeldia Morris Eller. Five children become their older brother's "army" as they work together to keep their family intact during a time of crisis for their mother. 07–7862 $2.95.

WILD CHILD by Mari Hanes. A heartrending story of a young boy who was abandoned and struggled alone for survival. You will be moved as you read how one woman's love tames this boy who was more animal than human. 07–8224 $2.95.

THE SURGEON'S FAMILY by David Hernandez with Carole Gift Page. This is an incredible three-generation story of a family that has faced danger and death—and has survived. Walking dead-end streets of violence and poverty, often seemingly without hope, the family of David Hernandez has struggled to find a new kind of life. 07–6684 $2.95.

The books listed are available at your bookstore. If unavailable, send check with order to cover retail price plus 10% for postage and handling to:

Tyndale House Publishers, Inc.
Box 80
Wheaton, Illinois 60189

Prices and availability subject to change without notice. Allow 4-6 weeks for delivery.